Jessi's Horrible Prank

**Other books by
Ann M. Martin**

Rachel Parker, Kindergarten Show-off
Eleven Kids, One Summer
Ma and Pa Dracula
Yours Turly, Shirley
Ten Kids, No Pets
Slam Book
Just a Summer Romance
Missing Since Monday
With You and Without You
Me and Katie (the Pest)
Stage Fright
Inside Out
Bummer Summer

BABY-SITTERS LITTLE SISTER series
THE BABY-SITTERS CLUB mysteries
THE BABY-SITTERS CLUB series
(see back of book for a more complete listing)

Jessi's Horrible Prank

Ann M. Martin

AN
APPLE
PAPERBACK

SCHOLASTIC INC.
New York Toronto London Auckland Sydney

For Alexandra, Taylor, and Daniel

No part of this publication may be reproduced in whole or in part, or stored in a retrieval system, or transmitted in any form or by any means, electronic, mechanical, photocopying, recording, or otherwise, without written permission of the publisher. For information regarding permission, write to Scholastic Inc., 555 Broadway, New York, NY 10012.

ISBN 0-590-47013-2

12 11 10 9 8 7 6 5 4 3 2 1   4 5 6 7 8 9/9

Printed in the U.S.A.   40

First Scholastic printing, May 1994

The author gratefully acknowledges
Peter Lerangis
for his help in
preparing this manuscript.

Jessi's Horrible Prank

CHAPTER 1

"*G*irl, what *are* you doing?"

Uh-oh. I had thought I was alone in the hallway. Instead I was caught red-handed by a classmate of mine, Sanjita Batts. Actually, red-*toed* was more like it. I confess, I was walking to my Short Takes class *en pointe*.

That is ballet terminology for "on the tips of your toes." And I mean the very tips. It's hard to do, especially for a sixth-grader like me.

Walking *en pointe* looks beautiful on stage. But in the hallway of Stoneybrook Middle School, it looks . . . well, dumb.

So why was I doing it? Because I, Jessica Ramsey, am a dance fanatic. I *love* ballet and I want to be a professional dancer someday. Even if it means having mangled toes the rest of my life. (Have you ever *seen* a ballerina's feet? They're frightening.)

"Just practicing," I said, lowering myself to a normal walking position.

"Don't stop." Sanji had a mischievous glint in her eye. "You should walk into class like that!"

"No way!" I replied.

"Seriously! Can you imagine the look on Mr. Trout's face?"

I couldn't help giggling. We have a new Short Takes teacher every term, and our latest one, Mr. Trout, was kind of a nerd.

Every student at Stoneybrook Middle School has Short Takes for one period a day. It's a special program of revolving courses. No, the room does not turn in a slow circle like one of those fancy hotel restaurants. What I mean is, every grading period we get a new subject and a new teacher. What kind of subjects? Unusual ones, like Stress Reduction for Teens; or Project Work, in which we all had to take after-school jobs in the community (I worked in a movie theater).

Our current class was called Software from Scratch, which was really another way of saying Computer Programming.

Computer programs are a little like dances. On the outside they both look fun and easy. But behind every graceful ballet is a lot of sweating and grunting and muscle strain and step-by-step memorizing. And behind every cool graphics program is a million or so lines of gobbledygook.

That's what our Short Takes class was about. Creating the gobbledygook.

Yawn. Give me an hour a day of dance warmups *anytime*.

As Sanjita and I headed to class, we heard the loud clattering of high heels from around the corner ahead of us.

"Quick," Sanji whispered. "Dolly One or Two?"

"Um . . . Two," I said.

I was wrong. Ms. Bernhardt, otherwise known as Dolly One, bounced around the corner toward us. Her thick blonde hair looked as if it were doing jumping jacks on her head.

Dolly Two is another teacher, Ms. Vandela. The two Dollies, as you can guess, look alike. They're short and big-chested. They both have huge smiles and Major Hair that cascades in ringlets over their shoulders. They also wear tons of makeup. You've probably already figured out how they got their nicknames. Right. They're both Dolly Parton clones — and Dolly Parton *fans*, so they don't mind their nicknames at all. (In case you don't know, Dolly Parton is a famous country-western singer who fits the above description.)

"Hi, girls!" Dolly One chirped as she bustled by with a clipboard. "I'm posting sign-up sheets for the Follies."

"Already?" Sanji asked.

"It's springtime, darling," Dolly One replied. "Now, I want both of you to think about signing up. We want to get a good cross section of the school!"

"Okay," Sanji said.

I should explain something. Sanjita is Puerto Rican and I am African-American. Stoneybrook is a mostly white town. What Dolly One meant by *cross section* was "not only white students."

Now, I knew she was only trying to be fair. She's a nice person, and she wanted to make sure Sanji and I didn't feel excluded. But statements like that make me feel funny. They remind me how different I am in some people's eyes.

I didn't always feel so different. In Oakley, New Jersey, where I grew up, people of all colors lived together and no one made a big deal about it. But when my family moved to Stoneybrook before sixth grade started, boy, were we in for a shock. Some people were really cold to us, as if we didn't belong. Others seemed afraid to be near us. Kids acted hostile to me in school. It was *awful* for awhile. Fortunately, things have improved a lot since then. Stoneybrook has turned out to be a great place, and I made a bunch of the best friends in the world when I joined the Baby-sitters Club (which I'll tell you about later).

Anyway, I was dying to find out about the show. As Ms. Bernhardt clickety-clacked down the hallway, I asked Sanjita, "What are the Follies?"

"You know, the Sixth-Grade Follies?" Sanji said. "Where the sixth-graders make up songs and skits and stuff? SMS has one every year."

I shrugged. "I didn't live here last year."

"Well, it's *sooo* hilarious. My big sister was in last year's. The students write the whole show. You get to do imitations and make fun of teachers, students, the school — everything." Then she laughed and added, "Probably even walk on your toes, if you want."

"Are you going to sign up?" I asked.

"No way. I get stage fright. You?"

"I might."

Might? Whoa. An end-of-the-year show, all original stuff — it sounded perfect. I *love* to make people laugh. I was the comedy highlight of a school production of *Peter Pan* (well, I was). And with my dance experience, maybe I'd be able to choreograph and perform.

I was flying high as we walked into our Short Takes class.

Mr. Trout was scribbling something on the

blackboard. His eyes darted toward Sanji and me.

"Hello, Mr. Trout," Sanji said in a voice that was so friendly it sounded phony.

He looked back at the board, adjusted his glasses, and grunted a soft "Hi."

Sanji glanced at me, rolled her eyes, and giggled. We both sat down as the bell rang.

To my right, John Rosen and Mark O'Connell were playing tic-tac-toe, passing a sheet of paper back and forth. To my left, Sandra Hart was reading a comic book. A spitball flew across the room and landed in Renee Johnson's hair. Two boys burst out laughing.

"*Ewww!*" Renee shouted. "That's disgusting! Mr. Trout, Craig and George are throwing spitballs."

Mr. Trout turned around. Instead of looking angry or annoyed, he looked . . . lost. If you didn't know he was a teacher, you'd think he was scared that Craig and George would scold *him*. "Uh, that's enough, now," he said, twirling the chalk in his fingers. "Okay?"

The two boys just giggled again. The rest of my classmates were barely holding in their laughter. Sanjita's hand was over her mouth and she was turning purple.

I admit, I had the urge to laugh, too. You have to picture Mr. Trout. He's about six feet tall and extremely skinny, with this waxy black hair combed in a style right out of the 1970s. His pants are too big and always bagging over his Hush Puppies. He alternates two tweed jackets from day-to-day, which he wears over old tattersall shirts that have plastic pocket protectors.

What's worse, sometimes he pronounces his *r*'s a little like *w*'s. Just slightly, though, and only when he's *extremely* nervous.

But the way some kids were acting, you'd think he was Elmer Fudd.

"All right, can anyone come to the board and write the last lines of this program?" Mr. Trout asked.

From the back of the class, I could hear Maria Fazio whisper, "Wite the wast wines of this pwogwam?"

A few kids around her cracked up. John and Mark snickered and kept playing tic-tac-toe. Sandra buried her face in her comic book. Sanjita let out a big yawn. No one volunteered.

I couldn't believe how rude they all were. Any other teacher would have yelled, or made a joke like "Don't all speak up at once," or called on someone to answer the question.

Not Mr. Trout. He just fidgeted and looked helpless.

My good mood was taking a nosedive.

His nervousness was making *me* nervous. I wanted to raise my hand, but I would have looked so dorky.

As the class began settling down, Sanjita passed me a note that looked like this:

I tried to stifle a laugh. It came out sounding like a pig snort. Very elegant.

Well, needless to say, the class went by slowly. Fortunately, though, everyone settled down. And I managed to stay awake right till the end.

Short Takes is my third-period class. Five periods later, school was over. But before leaving, I had to make two stops. The first was the main hallway, where I signed my name on the Follies sheet. (At the bottom was an announcement that the first planning meeting would be on Thursday, only three days away.)

As I was writing, I heard a familar voice say, "Ooh, you're going to be in the show! Great! You will be *sooo* funny!"

"Hi, Mal!" I replied.

Mallory Pike is my very best friend ever. We can talk about *anything*. (Plus she laughs at all my jokes.) She's the only person I know who's as crazy about horse stories as I am. Marguerite Henry books, *The Black Stallion* series, *The Saddle Club* — we've read them all. Someday we'll be talking about her own books, guaranteed. She is an incredibly talented writer and illustrator.

"Are you going to sign up?" I asked.

"I'll just watch," she said.

Mal doesn't like performing. During a school production of *Peter Pan*, she was in charge of costumes. She also just recovered from a case of mono, so I guess she wanted to take it easy.

Together we walked to my second stop, the front steps of the school. That's where our BSC friends always meet to chat at the end of the day.

We walked into a very serious conversation between Claudia Kishi and Kristy Thomas.

"I would never do it," Kristy was saying,

arms folded tightly. "Not in a million years."

"I would," Claudia replied. "I mean, I *might*. Just for fun."

"Fun? It would be *permanent*, Claud. No going back. What happens years from now, when you have to look for a job?"

Claudia laughed. "You don't wear it. Who's going to know?"

"What if they just happen to look up your nostrils?" Kristy asked.

"Gross, Kristy."

I couldn't help barging in. "What are you guys *talking* about?"

"Nose rings," Kristy replied. "Can you believe it? Claud wants to have her nose pierced."

"Kristy, I didn't say I *wanted* to," Claudia insisted. "All I said was nose jewelry looks cool."

"Oh, yeah, great," Kristy replied, "if you want to look like Elsie the Cow."

Claudia rolled her eyes. "You get the *side* of your nose pierced, not the middle."

"Who looks like Elsie the Cow?"

We all turned at the sound of Mary Anne Spier's voice. She was walking toward us with Stacey McGill. "No one," I said. "Yet."

"Mooooo," moaned Claudia. She had taken off one of her clip-on earrings and somehow clasped it onto her nose.

We all burst out laughing. Claudia quickly took the earring off and wrinkled her nose. "Yeow, that hurts. I changed my mind."

"Good," Kristy said. She looked at her watch, then at the line of buses out front. "Oops. See you guys later!"

" 'Bye!" we all called out as she sprinted for her bus.

Stoneybrook is part suburban, part rural, and part ritzy. Most of us live in the suburban part, within walking distance from the school, but Kristy lives in a mansion, way across town on the ritzy side. (Kristy, however, is about as unritzy as can be. Her stepfather is a millionaire, which is a long story I'll leave for later.)

The rest of us began walking home, discussing nose jewelry. I think it's great, but let's face it, it takes awhile for some African styles to catch on. Claudia was really the only other one who liked the idea. Stacey admitted it looked okay, but only on other people.

When I got home, my aunt Cecelia was out front, looking very cross. (She's my dad's sister, and she lives with us.) My sister Becca, who's eight, was running around from behind the house.

"I can't find him, Aunt Cecelia," Becca said.

"Oh my lord, that boy will be the death of

me!" Aunt Cecelia replied. *"John Philip! Where are you?"*

"Squirt!" Becca called out.

John Philip and Squirt are the same person, my baby brother. He popped out from behind a rhododendron bush, yelling, "Worrrr!"

"Aaah! A dinosaur!" Becca squealed.

Squirt shrieked with excitement. Then he raised his hands over his head and repeated, "Worrrr!" (That's his way of roaring.)

My brother is a toddler. He is the cutest child alive. Aunt Cecelia is about fifty or so. Cute is not the word I'd use to describe her. *Severe*, maybe. She moved in with us to take care of Squirt when my mom went back to work. Boy, was it hard to get used to her. She's loosened up since then, but she can still be a pain sometimes. The strange thing is, my dad is about the most easygoing man in the world. Oh, well, I guess Aunt Cecelia has enough sourness for two people.

She was scowling at Squirt, her hands firmly on her hips. "Young man, I do not want to see you hiding behind those bushes again."

"He can't understand you, Aunt Cecelia," I volunteered.

"Dess-seee!" Squirt shrieked, toddling toward me with wide open arms.

"Hi, Squirt! Hi, everyone!" I called out.

"Oh, he most certainly can!" Aunt Cecelia replied. "They understand much more than you think!" Then, as an afterthought, she added, "Hello, Jessica."

I scooped up Squirt and nuzzled him on his belly. He giggled uncontrollably and then said, "Ah-*den*!" (That's *again* in his private language, which we call Squirt-glish.)

"Sandwich!" Becca yelled. She wrapped her arms around me, trapping our brother between us. "We're the bread and Squirt is the peanut butter!"

That made Squirt wriggle *and* giggle. Aunt Cecelia shook her head and said, "Honestly, you girls spoil him."

But I could see the sides of her mouth curling up into a smile.

Squirt squirmed out from between the pieces of bread and screamed, "Duck, duck, doose!"

Well, we played that about a hundred times. Then we played hide-and-seek, but Squirt kept hiding in the same two places. Afterward he wanted to be lifted up like a "heckopper" (helicopter). That's when Aunt Cecelia gave up.

By five o'clock we were still playing. Well, Squirt was. I was exhausted.

Honk! Honk!

Daddy's car pulled into the driveway. He

had picked up Mama, and they were both giving us these huge smiles from the front seat.

"Day-eee! Mummumm!" Squirt began running toward the car.

"Careful!" Aunt Cecelia called out from the front porch.

Squirt fell forward on the lawn. He immediately sat up and stared at his hands, which were covered with freshly cut grass.

"Blind-side tackle!" Daddy bellowed as he got out of the car. He fell to the ground and wrestled with Squirt, who screamed with joy.

Becca and I joined the pileup. Mama leaned over us and managed to kiss us all.

"John! Your shirt!" Aunt Cecelia warned.

Daddy sat up. Blades of grass clung to his white shirt, along with thin green stains.

He pretended to be shocked and looked around at all of us. "Who did this to me? Do you realize how much work Aunt Cecelia is going to have to do? Arrrrgh!"

He sprang to his feet and began chasing us around the yard.

Among our shrieks and giggles, I could hear Aunt Cecelia's voice saying, "How much work *who's* going to do?"

I thought Mama was going to die laughing.

Welcome to the Ramsey family.

CHAPTER 2

"Remember Mr. Steinmetz?" Claudia asked.

Kristy and Mary Anne howled. "He was a custodian," Mary Anne explained, "who had a missing front tooth."

"Every time he said an *S*, he whistled," Kristy went on. "Like, Misshhhhter Shhhtein-metshhh — oh, I can't do it."

"But Alan Gray could!" Claudia chimed in.

Kristy mumbled, "That's the one thing he's good for." (Alan Gray is Eighth-Grade Enemy Number One.)

"Well, he did the funniest imitation," Mary Anne said. "I thought I'd never stop laughing — but I felt so *awful*!"

"Oh, Mr. Steinmetz didn't mind," Kristy reminded her. "He laughed so hard he almost keeled over on the floor."

It was 5:28 that Monday afternoon, the day I'd signed up for the Follies. Our Baby-sitters

Club meeting was about to begin, and guess what we were talking about?

The Follies of two years ago. I had walked into Claudia's bedroom (the BSC headquarters) talking about our Follies with Mallory. That was when Kristy, Claudia, and Mary Anne started telling us *their* experiences.

Those three, by the way, are part of The Big Four, the first BSC members. (The Fourth is Stacey.)

Actually the club began with the Big *One*, Kristy.

Okay, I said I'd tell you all about the BSC, so here goes:

A History of the Baby-sitters Club
by Jessica Ramsey

It was a dark and stormy night in Stoney-brook, Connecticut. Time and time again, a telephone receiver slammed in the Thomas house. "Woe is me," cried Mrs. Thomas, "for I cannot find a suitable person to watch over my youngest offspring, and my three eldest are unavailable tonight."

Alas, my heart aches to see my mother in such distress, thought Kristy. *Alone with four children, abandoned by a husband (my father), and deserving of a night out. Oh, if only there were a single phone number at which she might reach a group of reliable sitters.*

Kristy stood up, struck by an inspiration.

Quickly she called her two best friends, Claudia Kishi and Mary Anne Spier.

"Hark! Hear my plan," announced Kristy to each. "Let us meet regularly — Monday, Wednesday, and Friday, between 5:30 and 6:00. Let us elect officers, and have a telephone! Henceforth, at those appointed times, the parents in our fair village may secure the services of whoever shall join me in this historic enterprise."

"I shall ask my friend Stacey to join," said Claudia.

With exclamations of joy and triumph, the Baby-sitters Club was born. Quickly its fame grew, and the club expanded to nine members. Stoneybrook lived happily ever after, as did Mrs. Thomas, who married a millionaire.

The End

Well, *something* like that.

In plain English, the BSC meets to take phone calls from parents who need sitters. With so many members, we can cover almost all job requests. Parents are happy because they know they'll get a good sitter with just one call. *We're* happy because we get lots of jobs.

All from the amazing mind of Kristy.

And I do mean amazing. You could put her in the desert and she'd figure out how to make it rain. She's constantly dreaming up ways to solve problems. She didn't just invent the BSC; she set up all the rules and traditions, including (1) a record book that contains a job calendar, a list of clients (complete with addresses, phone numbers, and rates paid), and a description of our charges' likes and dislikes; (2) a notebook in which we write about our job experiences; and (3) Kid-Kits, which are small toy- and game-filled boxes we sometimes take with us on sitting jobs.

What's Kristy like? Short and loud (well, she *is*). But also friendly and down-to-earth, even though, as I mentioned, she lives in the ritzy section of Stoneybrook. She has plain brown hair, and she *lives* in jeans and sweats. She's also a terrific athlete. And she doesn't just play sports, she coaches, too — a team called Kristy's Krushers, which she organized herself. It's made up of kids too young or too klutzy or too shy for Little League. They play another team, Bart's Bashers, which is coached by Bart Taylor.

Bart and Kristy are an item. (I can't say anymore. Kristy would kill me.)

You would not believe the size of Kristy's house. It never feels crowded, even though ten people live in it. Yes, *ten*. Watson Brewer, Kristy's stepfather, has two kids from a prior marriage (Karen and Andrew), who live there every other month. When Kristy, her mom, and her three brothers (seventeen-year-old Charlie, fifteen-year-old Sam, and seven-year-old David Michael) moved in, that made eight. Then Kristy's parents adopted a little girl named Emily Michelle (who's two) and Kristy's grandmother (Nannie) moved in. (Ten.)

Click.

Claudia's digital clock flipped to 5:30. In the middle of a sentence, Kristy interrupted herself to say, "This meeting will come to order!"

Did you figure out that Kristy is the BSC president? She is. And she hardly ever misses the click of 5:30. I bet, for the rest of her life, she will say "Order!" at 5:30 on Mondays, Wednesdays, and Fridays.

"Any new business?" Kristy asked.

Claudia, who had been passing around a huge bag of tortilla chips, thrust it toward Kristy. "Try these."

Kristy grabbed a fistful of chips and shoved some in her mouth. "Pooey goo," she mumbled.

"Say it, don't spray it," Stacey McGill said, pretending (I think) to wipe off some damp chip pieces.

Kristy swallowed. "Pretty good."

"They're baked, not fried," Claudia remarked. "Which means you can eat, like, three times as many."

Grinning, she reached under her bed and pulled out two more bags.

Claud's room is the official BSC headquarters (because she has her own phone), but a better name for it might be *hide*-quarters. You can't pick up a thing in there without discovering candy, cookies, chips, pretzels, or Nancy Drew books. She hides them because her parents allow only Wholesome Foods and Great Literature in the house. (Silly, huh? As Claudia says, "There's more to life than *Johnny Tremain* and brussels sprouts.")

Claudia once thought she was adopted (untrue), because she is so different from the rest of her straitlaced family. They're all smart (her older sister, Janine, is a certified genius), and none of them is interested in art. Claud's a pretty rotten student but a fabulous artist — in watercolor, sculpture, drawing, *everything*. (Maybe she gets her artistic inspiration from eating all that junk food.)

Can you picture Claudia? Obese, huh? Nope. She looks like a model, thin and blemish-free. (I don't know how she does it.) She has the most gorgeous Japanese features, silky black hair, and almond-shaped eyes. Plus she always puts together the coolest outfits, mostly from stuff she finds in flea markets. For example, at that meeting she was wearing '50s-style cat's-eye glasses frames, a plastic barrette in the shape of an alligator, a tie-dyed T-shirt, and bell-bottoms. And it looked fantastic.

Officially, Claudia is the BSC vice-president, although she could be called Chief Sugar Supplier or something.

Not for everybody, though. One of our members, Stacey, cannot eat sweets. She's a diabetic, which means her body is unable to regulate the amount of sugar in her bloodstream. So she has to give herself (warning: if you have a weak stomach, skip to the next paragraph) daily injections of something called insulin.

Which is why Claudia also stocks up on pretzels, chips, and other sugar-free goodies.

Stacey is one of the BSC's three blondes. She's also our *only* math whiz, so she gets to be treasurer. Lucky her. She listens to us moan and groan as we give her our dues every Monday (yuck). Then she divides up the money for our expenses — helping Claudia pay her phone bill, restocking our Kid-Kits, and so on.

Like Claud, Stacey's a stunning dresser. Unlike Claud, she wouldn't be caught dead in a flea market. She likes up-to-the-minute fashions. "Urban chic," she once described her style (sounds snobby, I know — but she's not). She grew up in New York City, the fashion capital of the world — and the dance capital, if you ask me. And theater, and restaurant, and museum . . . do I sound jealous? I am. I ♥ the Big Apple!

How did Stacey end up in Stoneybrook? Well, first her dad's job brought her family here. Then her dad's job took them back to NYC. Then her parents divorced, and Stacey moved back here with her mom.

Confusing? Well, it isn't ideal, but it has its good points: Stacey gets to live here *plus* visit her dad in New York. (And sometimes we get to go with her.)

Mary Anne Spier is our other Big Apple freak. She's the only non-New Yorker I know who has mastered the subway system.

That's not surprising, because Mary Anne is the world's most organized person. As BSC secretary, she has to be. Her job is to handle the record book. The moment a request comes in, Mary Anne has to know (1) who is available, (2) who has conflicts (doctor appointments, ballet classes, and so on), and (3) how to assign jobs fairly, so everyone gets a roughly equal share. Then she records the job on the official calendar. (And she has never, ever made a mistake.)

Mary Anne is Kristy's best friend. They actually look similar — petite, with brown hair and dark eyes — but their personalities couldn't be more different. Mary Anne is shy and sensitive, and she hates sports. She cries at the slightest thing. She's read *Wuthering Heights* three times, and the pages of her book are blistered from teardrops.

Mary Anne's life is sort of like a sad novel with a happy ending. Her mom died when she was a baby. Mr. Spier was too devastated to care for Mary Anne, so he sent her away to her grandparents — and then he had to fight to get her back. To prove he could be a good single parent, he raised Mary Anne very strictly. For years she had an early curfew and had to dress in little-girl clothing. But one day, when Mary Anne was in seventh grade, a new girl moved to Stoneybrook and changed Mary Anne's life. Her name was Dawn Schafer and she came from California. Her parents had just divorced, and her mom had decided to move back to her own hometown, Stoneybrook. Well, Dawn joined the Baby-sitters Club — and she and Mary Anne discovered that Mr. Spier and Mrs. Schafer were high-school sweethearts! And guess who fell in love again?

Dum-dum-de-dum! (Wedding bells.)

After the wedding, Mary Anne and her dad moved into the Schafers' rambling old farmhouse. All of a sudden Mary Anne had a mom, a big new house, a happy and less strict dad, and a stepsister who was in the BSC. What a perfect ending . . . almost. The only trouble is, Dawn recently got incredibly homesick for California, so now she's back there for an extended visit.

We *all* miss her. Dawn is wonderful. She's really committed to some serious causes — the environment, health, and fighting sexism. She eats only health foods: organic veggies and fruits, no red meats, no sweets. I admire her, even though I'll take a nice juicy hamburger over tofu anytime.

Dawn (when she's here) is the BSC's alternate officer, which means she takes over when anyone's absent. She's blonde, but her hair is much lighter than Stacey's. Out in California, she belongs to a baby-sitting organization called the We ♥ Kids Club. (*All* the members are health-food eaters. They would have heart attacks if Claudia moved to California.)

All the BSCers I just mentioned are eighth-graders, two years older than Mallory and me. We young uns are called junior members. We don't have official responsibilities, and because both our sets of parents think we're babies, we can't take late sitting jobs. (Grrrr.) Actually, it's not too awful. The club gets plenty of requests for afternoon and weekend jobs.

Lots of those jobs are at Mal's house. Did I tell you Mal has *seven* younger siblings, including a set of triplets? It's true. Baby-sitting at her house is like going to a circus.

Okay. Now you know that (a) the BSC is very busy, and (b) we've lost one member to California. You may be wondering how we cope with this problem. Leave it to Kristy. Soon after the club started, she decided we should have *associate* members. They fill in during emergencies but don't have to attend meetings or pay dues.

One of our associates, Shannon Kilbourne, has become Dawn's "pinch-hitter" (in the words of Coach Kristy). Shannon, who lives across the street from Kristy, goes to a private school called Stoneybrook Day School. She's involved in lots of extracurricular activities there, but somehow she manages to take plenty of sitting jobs, too. Shannon has really thick, curly, dark blonde hair and blue eyes.

Our other associate member is a guy. Well, not just any guy. He's Mary Anne's boyfriend, Logan Bruno. I guess he's cute. Everybody says he is. He *is* a terrific sitter, but he tries to keep a low profile because his friends make fun of him. I hope they'll grow out of it someday, but you know boys.

Anyway, back to our meeting.

Rrriing!

"Hello, Baby-sitters Club!" Claudia said, picking up the receiver. "Hi, Dr. Johanssen. . . . Sure. I'll call you right back."

She hung up and turned to Mary Anne.

"Three weeks from Wednesday for Charlotte Johanssen?"

"Three weeks?" Shannon exclaimed.

"You know Char's mom — *turbo*-organized," Stacey replied.

Mary Anne looked up from the record book. "Everyone's free. Want to do it, Stace?" (Stacey and Charlotte are very close.)

"Shhhhtashhhhey?" Kristy said, trying to whistle her *S*'s.

"Okay, Mr. Steinmetz," Stacey said, cracking up.

Claudia shook her head. "All those in favor of getting Alan Gray in here to give Kristy some lessons, say aye."

"Aye!" Mallory, Stacey, Mary Anne, Shannon, and I yelled.

"Aaughh!" Kristy screamed. "I'll never do it again! I promise!"

And she didn't.

But her imitation got me thinking again. Of the Follies.

Or I should say, The SMS Annual Sixth-Grade Follies, Starring Jessica Ramsey!

Well, I could dream, couldn't I?

CHAPTER 3

EXACLY 10 MINS
BEFORE THE END OF CLASS,
WE WILL ALL DORP OUR
BOOKS ON THE FLOOR AT
THE SAME TIME.
PASS THIS NOTE ON!!!!!!!!!

Oh, groan.

I stared at the note Janet O'Neal had passed me. This was stupid. The oldest trick in the book.

Every day the pranks in my Short Takes class were getting worse. The day before, Wednesday, half the class had turned its back on Mr. Trout at John Rosen's signal. Thursday was Mr. Trout's ninth day as our teacher. At this rate they'd be tarring and feathering him by next week.

The worst part was watching Mr. Trout react. Sometimes he'd give a small, phony laugh. Other times he'd sigh and look slightly annoyed. But most of the time he did absolutely nothing.

That just made everybody braver. Even Justine Moss, the shyest girl in the class, had joined in the back-turning prank.

It was awful. Dweeb or no dweeb, Mr. Trout was a human. He had to have feelings, even though he didn't show them. He was bound to break sooner or later. Part of me hoped he would get angry and keep the whole class for detention. That would stop the fooling around.

Mr. Trout turned to the class, pointing to a short program he'd written. "Who wants to tell me how to debug this?"

"With de fly swatter?" Mark O'Connell called out.

Giggles all around.

"Come *on*, guys!" protested Renee Johnson.

"Come on, guys," Craig Avazian imitated, in a high-pitched voice.

"Mr. Trout, he's making fun of me!" Renee said.

"Mr. Trout, he's making fun of me!" Craig repeated.

Ugh.

This went on for awhile, until Renee just stopped talking. By the time Mr. Trout tried to draw our attention back to the blackboard, I'd forgotten what the program was about.

"Pass it on, Jessi!" hissed Janet behind me.

Oops. I still had the note. I tapped the guy in front of me, Jimmy Bouloukos, on the shoulder and gave it to him. He laughed and immediately slipped it to the next person.

For the rest of the class, I could not concentrate. The examples on the board looked like hieroglyphics. All around me, kids were staring at the clock. Mr. Trout gave up calling on volunteers and just lectured the whole time. My mind kept wandering to the Sixth-Grade Follies meeting, which was going to be held after school.

At fourteen minutes before the end of class,

Mr. Trout was droning on about things called hexadecimals.

At thirteen minutes, he started writing on the blackboard.

At twelve, he was still writing. Kids were quietly piling up their books. Renee looked absolutely disgusted.

At eleven, even Renee was gathering her books.

That day, Sanjita was sitting right behind me. I could feel her staring at me quizzically. She tapped me on my back, as if to say, "Don't forget."

I was now the only person not getting ready. Twenty other kids surrounded me, fingers wrapped around neat piles of books. The clock's second hand was sweeping around, approaching the final time.

Imagine how I felt.

Not doing anything would be like betraying my classmates. If they were kept for detention, and *I* went free, I'd never hear the end of it.

But that was a big *if.* Chances were Mr. Trout wouldn't do anything. Then I'd have to explain why I was too chicken to go along.

Ease up, Jessi, I told myself. It's just a joke.

The second hand was passing 9 on the clock. Fifteen seconds to go.

With a sigh, I quickly shuffled all my stuff together.

Five . . . four . . . three . . . two . . . one . . .
WHAAAAAAMMM!

The books hit the floor like a bomb.

Mr. Trout squealed. That is the only way to describe the sound he made. He leaped off the ground, too, and his chalk flew out of his hand.

Then . . . he screamed at the top of his lungs, made us pick up each book with our teeth, and took us all to the principal's office.

Wrong.

This is what he really did: First he adjusted his glasses. Then he cleared his throat. Finally he picked up the shattered pieces of chalk from the floor, took the largest chunk, and went right back to the program on the board.

No scolding, no detention, no nothing.

Maria started snickering, then Craig and John. Before long Renee was laughing, too.

And so was I. I couldn't help it.

Not because it was so funny. It wasn't, really. It was kind of sad. I guess I was laughing out of relief that Mr. Trout hadn't blown up.

At the end of class, Mr. Trout didn't even look up from his desk as we filed out.

A few kids gathered in the hallway to gloat about the prank. Not me. I wanted to get away from there as fast as possible.

The rest of the day flew by. At the sound

of the end-of-school bell, I ran to the auditorium.

The two Dollies were busily setting up a VCR and a TV on a portable cart.

I was the first student there.

"Jessi, hi!" Ms. Bernhardt (Dolly One) greeted me. "Do you know anything about plugging in VCRs?"

"I think I figured it out," Ms. Vandela (Dolly Two) announced.

I joined them behind the cart. Ms. Vandela was muttering, "Now, VCR In goes to TV Out, right?"

"Right!" Ms. Bernhardt and I chimed in.

Ms. Vandela held out a red wire. "So where does this go?"

Ms. Bernhardt shrugged. "Just hold onto it, Dolly Sister. When we turn it on, see what happens to your perm."

The two of them cracked up.

I knew I was going to enjoy this. The Dollies were fun.

More students filed into the auditorium, and a couple of kids who were real techies came to help us out. Then, when it was all set up, Ms. Bernhardt quieted the group down and gave a little speech.

About twenty of us had gathered. We were all bunched together in seats near the TV.

"Welcome, everybody!" Ms. Bernhardt said.

"Now, Ms. Vandela and I are new to the Follies this year, but we both have a little experience in theater — and we're determined to make this year's show the best in history!"

We all cheered.

"And to start things off right, we're going to show you a video with excerpts from last year's show. Roll 'em!"

Well, that video was one of the funniest things I had ever seen. One group of kids did a skit called "Gym for Teachers." Wearing potbellies, fake mustaches, and clodhopper shoes, they imitated SMS teachers huffing and puffing in gym class.

Kate Condos led a number called "The SMS Rap," during which she pulled our principal, Mr. Taylor, from the audience, and made him dance along. Another kid did a comedy routine, and a group of four performed a great tap number.

I was *psyched*.

By the end of the video, the whole group was bubbling with excitement.

Ms. Vandela took over then. "We have some special plans," she announced. "For the first time, the Sixth-Grade Follies will be a benefit. We'll be charging admission, and donating the profits to a worthy organization. This means we'll need two important committees.

"The performance committee will be in

charge of planning the show," Ms. Vandela continued. "That means deciding on a title and theme, figuring out the format, writing the material, helping to audition performers, and setting up subcommittees — like makeup and lighting. I must stress, though, that we want *everyone* to audition, even committee members."

A couple of kids groaned.

"It's just so we can get an idea of everyone's talent, that's all," Ms. Bernhardt said. "Very low pressure. Now, the *finance* committee will choose the charity we'll donate our proceeds to, plus organize the collection of money. May I have hands for the performance committee?"

I raised mine.

"Finance?"

I raised it again.

Ms. Bernhardt wrote me down for both.

I could not wait to begin work.

CHAPTER 4

"After much consideration blah blah bell curve mumble mumble perhaps the difficulty level exceeded expectations blah blah."

That wasn't exactly what Mr. Trout said. But it was something like that. I think he was trying to explain that we'd all flunked our first quiz.

Yes, quiz.

It had been a total surprise. Last Friday, he had passed out mimeographed sheets of computer gobbledygook. "A simple BASIC program," he had called it. (Or was it a "basic SIMPLE program"?)

Well, it wasn't either — simple *or* basic. I didn't understand a thing. I thought he'd made a mistake and given us a test in Ancient Greek.

I was horrified. Afterward, I talked to some classmates. It turned out *no one* had known how to answer the problems.

Now we were all facing the consequences.

Mr. Trout fiddled with a mechanical pencil, then tucked it behind his left ear. "As a result of the low scores, I have decided to cancel everyone's grades and devote a few days to rigorous review."

Big mistake. I mean, it didn't sound like "wigowous weview" to me, but it must have to Maria Fazio, because she was having a cow in the back of the class.

I turned and gave her a Look. So did Renee and a couple of others.

Fortunately, a bunch of kids were cheering about the grade cancellation. Mr. Trout didn't seem to hear Maria.

Actually, he seemed preoccupied with something on his desk. Or something *not* on his desk. He looked under his grade book, which had all our quiz papers tucked into it. Then he bent down and scanned the floor.

"That's odd . . . " he said under his breath. "I just had it in my hand. . . ."

He reached into his pants pocket, then into his shirt pocket protector (which was empty).

He turned to the right, scratching his head. His mechanical pencil was facing us now, still nestled behind his ear.

Oops.

I began to raise my hand to tell him, but

Janet reached from behind me and pulled it down.

When I turned to face her, she was smiling. She put her finger to her lips to shush me.

Around us, kids were catching on. Everyone was trying hard not to crack up.

I faced forward again. Mr. Trout was sitting at his desk, rummaging through his drawer. A box of paper clips fell out onto the floor.

"Oh, dear . . ." he said.

He pushed the drawer closed and dropped to his knees.

Rrrrrrrip.

His tie had gotten caught in the drawer. It must have been old, because it tore right off at the collar.

"Oh!" Mr. Trout exclaimed.

This was too much. No one could hold it in. The whole class was whooping. It sounded like a laugh track on a sitcom.

Mr. Trout quickly took off what was left of his tie and began picking up the paper clips. I felt so bad for him. But my stomach was in knots from laughing. If only he would say something — chuckle, *anything* — this whole thing wouldn't be so embarrassing. Or so funny.

While Mr. Trout was kneeling, Jimmy Bouloukos sneaked up to the desk and swiped the grade book. He rushed back to his own desk and stuffed it inside.

When Mr. Trout finally stood up, his pencil was back in his pocket protector. Beads of sweat had formed just beneath his strange, thick hair. He dumped the paper clips back in his desk and said, "Now we can settle down to . . ."

His voice drifted off. He was staring at the desk again. No one said a word about Jimmy.

He opened his desk drawer again, looked inside, and closed it.

"Hmmm . . . um . . ." You could tell he was about to ask about the book, but thought better of it. He probably figured he'd left it somewhere obvious and didn't want to humiliate himself again.

I wanted to laugh. My stomach was convulsing.

Turning to the blackboard, Mr. Trout said, "Now then, let me write out the first problem. . . ."

Someone piped up, *"Twout!"* in the back of the class, more like a strange animal noise than a word.

Mr. Trout looked over his shoulder. "I beg your pardon? Does someone have a question?"

"Just had something between my teeth," George Weiss said (whatever *that* meant).

If I were George's teacher, I would have smacked him. Mr. Trout just nodded and turned back around.

Then someone else chimed in, *"Twout!"*

"You see," Mr. Trout said, either ignoring or not hearing the sound effects, "at this step, we must ensure the program does not result in an endless loop — "

"Twout!"

"Twout!"

Great. The class had turned into a pool of barking seals.

This kind of stuff continued the rest of the hour. At one point, when Mr. Trout was busy writing on the board, Jimmy returned the grade book.

If Mr. Trout was surprised, he didn't show it. He just kept trying to teach, as if nothing was wrong.

He never did give back those quizzes, which was probably just as well.

As I left class, I had a thought. Mr. Trout knew exactly what he was doing. He actually had a good sense of humor, and he was putting on an act. He figured that would make class less boring. He probably practiced that pencil-behind-the-ear routine in the teachers' lounge. Dollies One and Two coached him.

That *had* to be it. Why else would anyone act so strange?

I believed that theory for about one and a half minutes. Then I let myself forget about Mr. Trout and think about more important things.

Like the Sixth-Grade Follies finance committee. We were scheduled to meet after school, to talk about which charitable organizations we might want to donate our proceeds to. I was going to suggest this theater group in Stamford that trains hearing-impaired actors and puts on plays with sign-language accompaniment. (I had learned about them from the family of one of my favorite charges, Matt Braddock, who is profoundly deaf.)

I ended up seeing Mr. Trout twice more that day. The first time, I was rushing to lunch after gym. As I raced around a corner, I spotted him a few feet in front of me.

I slowed waaaay down. *No way* would I let him see me. What could I possibly say to him — "Duh, nice class today"?

Here's what I noticed, walking behind Mr. Trout. He stayed close to the wall. He had no bounce in his step at all. His hair sat on his head like a helmet. (I wondered if he used hair spray.)

At the cafeteria door, a group of three teachers was gabbing away. One of them, Mr. Dougherty, smiled at Mr. Trout as he passed, and nodded hello.

Mr. Trout must not have noticed. He walked right by without even looking in the teacher's direction. Mr. Dougherty just shrugged and plunged back into the conversation.

I guess Mr. Trout needed to learn some manners. Oh, well. He was new. And shy, maybe. No big deal.

I slipped into the cafeteria and hit the lunch line.

The second time I saw Mr. Trout was right before last period. I happened to pass by the teachers' lounge when I heard a laughing fit. I glanced inside to see four or five teachers sitting at a table, doubling over at something Mr. Williams was saying. I was dying to listen. They all looked as if they were having a great time.

That was when I noticed Mr. Trout. He was at another table, reading a book, facing away from the other teachers. As Mr. Williams went on, Mr. Trout hunched tighter over his book.

Now, I'm sorry, but *that* was weird in a major way. It wasn't just shy. It wasn't just bad manners, either.

I think Mr. Trout needed his own Short Takes course. In Human Relations.

After school I raced to my locker. I threw my books in and began pulling out what I needed to take home.

I was so wrapped up in thinking about the Follies, I almost didn't notice the conversation next to me.

Sanjita, Maria, and Sandra were at *their* lockers, not far from mine. They were giggling about something.

Before I closed my locker, I heard Maria say, "Of course it is! It's the most obvious one in the world!"

"You think so?" Sandra asked.

"I know so!" Maria insisted. "My uncle wears a toupee just like the Trout's. Haven't you noticed the gray hairs *just along the bottom*, where his real hair begins?"

"And how it never, ever bounces or falls across his face?" Sanjita added. "It's totally unnatural."

"I don't know," Sandra said. "It's a weird style and all, but it looks real to me."

"When was your last eye examination?" Maria asked.

"Ha ha," Sandra replied.

"There's got to be some way we can find out," Sanji said.

"We could ask him," Maria suggested.

I didn't stay to hear the rest. But they got me thinking.

I'd figured it was just hair spray. But they could have been right.

Poor Mr. Trout. Next thing you know, he'd turn out to have false teeth.

When I got to the auditorium, Ms. Vandela was about to close the door. "Wait!" I shouted.

I ran in. I took my seat. And all thoughts of toupees and weird teachers vanished from my mind.

CHAPTER 5

"Where are the pretzels?" I called out.

"I'll get them!" Becca replied.

She ran out of the kitchen. I dumped some potato chips into a bowl and reached into the refrigerator for a bunch of grapes. I added them to a fruit bowl that already had apples, oranges, and bananas.

I looked at the spread on the kitchen counter — potato chips, tortilla chips, fruit, M & M's, Triscuits, Goldfish, and (soon) pretzels. "Do you think this'll be enough?" I asked Mama.

"For seven sixth-graders?" Mama said. "I'll give it a half hour. But don't worry. Daddy's out back cleaning the barbecue."

It was 9:45 on Saturday morning, fifteen minutes before a meeting of the Follies performance committee. We'd already begun working on the script at school. Our title was *Hooray for Stoneywood!* In our "plot," SMS is really a school for celebrities in disguise.

This was our first meeting at my house. I was petrified. I wanted so badly to make a good impression.

Becca came rushing into the kitchen with a huge, open bag of pretzels. "Here!"

"Where were they?" Mama asked her.

"Oh . . . in my bedroom." She quickly added, "*Squirt* brought them there!"

"Uh-huh. Young lady, what are you going to do when your brother is old enough to defend himself?"

Becca ignored Mama's comment. "Jessi, do you want me to tape the meeting?"

"Tape it? Why?" I said.

"So you won't forget your ideas!" she replied. "Or I could just, like, listen and help out if you forget stuff."

Oh, boy. Becca Ramsey, show-biz brat in the making. "You can listen if you help me set up."

"Yeeeeaaaa!" Becca grabbed two bowls and ran into the living room.

We were ready by 9:57. At 10:03, the doorbell rang.

"I'll get it!" Becca screamed.

We both got there at the same time. Becca pulled the door open and said, "Hi! I'm Jessi's sister!"

It was Randy Rademacher, a guy I didn't know too well. His dad was standing with him.

"Hi," Randy said.

Randy's dad was looking around the living room, barely noticing my sister and me. "Are your parents home?" was the first thing he said.

Luckily, Mom came walking in at that moment. "Hello, there," she said sweetly. "I'm Jessi and Becca's mother. Nice to meet you."

Mr. Rademacher smiled and extended his hand. He looked relieved. "Hello, I'm Bill Rademacher. You have a lovely home."

"Thank you," Mama replied. "You're welcome to stay if you'd like. My husband's in the back preparing the grill."

"Oh, the kids'll be having lunch?" Mr. Rademacher asked.

"Yes, and we have plenty of burgers and hot dogs, so don't be shy."

"That's nice of you, but I've got some errands." He backed out the door. "Call me when you're ready, son."

Randy sank into the living room couch. He seemed a little nervous. Just as his father had seemed.

I offered Randy some chips and sat across from him.

"Am I the first one?" he asked.

"Uh-huh," I said. "But everyone's coming."

"Except Mara," Randy said. "I saw her in front of her house."

"Oh? Is she feeling all right?"

He shrugged. "She looked fine. She said she had to go to the mall with her mom."

"Uh-huh."

I didn't ask any questions. Mara Semple's okay, but her parents were awfully cold to us when we moved in.

I mean, I know it's not right to judge, and maybe Mara really did have something important to do. But people can be weird. It's hard to believe, but some people are very uncomfortable about being in African-Americans' houses. Uncomfortable? Scared is more like it sometimes.

Like Mr. Rademacher. He was being so wary when he was at the door. What did he expect to see?

I don't know. The whole thing is very unfair and very confusing.

Luckily, kids are usually much looser than parents. Randy, his mouth full of pretzels, was reaching into his backpack. "I have this great idea," he said.

Ding-dong!

"I'll get it!" Becca yelled.

During the next few minutes the rest of the committee arrived (minus Mara). Each one was greeted by our honorary mascot, my sister.

Randy was dying to show us something. He pulled some sunglasses, a comb, a small pillow, a toy microphone, and a box of raisins out of his pack. "Can I use your bathroom?" he asked.

"Sure.'" I showed him where it was, and he disappeared inside for about five minutes.

When he came out, his hair was slicked back and he was wearing the sunglasses. He'd tucked the pillow under his shirt, and he was holding the toy mike. He flashed us a smile.

Between his front teeth was a huge gap. It took me a couple of seconds to realize it was part of a raisin, smushed into the crack.

"Mr. Williams . . . as Elvis!" he shouted. Then he began wiggling and singing an off-pitch version of "Jailhouse Rock."

Well, we *screamed*. Mr. Williams does have slick hair, a pot belly, and a tooth gap. And he has that smooth, Elvis-style voice.

Next Bobby Gustavson gave me a script he'd been working on, based on *Wayne's World*. He played Wayne — and guess who volunteered to play Garth?

Me.

Okay, it wasn't typecasting. But it was hilarious.

We tried out a couple of other ideas, and

pretty soon we were rolling on the floor. Aunt Cecelia came in at one point and asked us if we'd lost our minds.

Randy took her hand and sang "I'm All Shook Up" as Elvis — and she actually *danced!* Whoa. I have never seen Aunt Cecelia loosen up *that* much.

Then, at noon, Daddy came in and said, "Barbecue's ready! Come and get it!"

You never saw a bunch of kids stand up so fast.

On our way to the back door, Randy said, "Ms. Bernhardt and Ms. Vandela are going to die when we show them this."

Then it hit me. The Perfect Idea. I didn't know why no one had thought of it before. I stopped right in the kitchen.

"The two Dollies!" I exclaimed. "We have to get some Dolly Parton wigs!"

"Yeah! And some, like, gigantic bras," suggested another committee member, Jamie Sperling, her face turning red.

"Here's the main plot: the Dollies are trying to put on the Sixth-Grade Follies," Randy said, "just like in real life — only the school is full of celebrities."

"The Folly Dollies!" exclaimed Justine Moss, who was also on the committee.

"Elvis darlin', y'all just have to tra out fuh the show," I drawled.

"Jessi, you've got to be one of them," Jamie said. "That would be *so* hilarious."

A black Dolly Parton? I guess that would be funny. Did I want to be laughed at because of that? Well . . .

"Maybe," I replied. "Unless they insist on playing themselves."

We gabbed away as we walked out to the backyard. Becca tagged along behind us, grinning like crazy.

If I didn't know better, I'd think she wanted to be in the show.

Well, she had three years to prepare. No harm in starting early.

Daddy's barbecue was amazing. We ate till we could hardly move.

My parents insisted on a preview of the show, which we gave them. They thought it was great.

I hoped the Dollies agreed.

CHAPTER 6

Sunday

Jessi and I sat for my brothers and
sisters today, and Becca came along.

Eight kids. And then
we had visitors. What
a job. Good thing
you recovered from
your mono, huh,
Mal? You would
not have believed
how well Mal
controlled the chaos!

Uh, Jessi, I'm supposed to be
the one who makes up the stories.

It's not a story.
It's just a — you
know...

An embellishment.
Right.

A *big* embellishment. But I had to do it. Kristy *makes* us write in that BSC notebook. I couldn't just tell the truth about our job. No one would believe it.

Let me start from the beginning.

You know how it is to sit for siblings. No matter how wonderful they are, they always manage to fight about something. Food, toys, tapes, TV shows, whatever. With three siblings, it's even worse. Four? Forget it.

Now try to imagine seven.

That's what it's like in the Pike house, twenty-four hours a day. You've heard of the Seven Dwarfs? Well, Mal's brothers and sisters are the Seven Terrors: Chaos, Disaster, Ruckus, Racket, Pandemonium, Turmoil, and Noise.

I usually take a bullhorn and a shield when I sit for them.

Okay, I'm exaggerating (a little). They're actually great kids. Besides, Mr. and Mrs. Pike always make sure to have two sitters. And Mal is usually one of them.

I was getting ready to go over there the day after the Follies committee meeting at my house. I was in a fabulous mood.

It's a good thing I was. Otherwise my sister would have driven me crazy — even *before* I went to the Pikes'.

I was still in my pj's when she ran into the kitchen. "Are you leaving yet?"

"No, silly," I said with a laugh. "Not dressed like this."

"Oh. Oops. Can I go with you?"

I took a box of cereal from the cabinet. "Well, I don't know if Mr. and Mrs. Pike would want that — "

"They would! They like me."

"I know they do, Becca. But when they're away from home — "

"Can't you call them? *I'll* call them! Come on, Jessi. I need someone to play with today!"

I let out a sigh. "What about going over to Charlotte's house?" (Charlotte Johanssen is Becca's best friend.)

"She's going to her grandparents'."

"All right," I said. "I'll call the Pikes as soon as I finish."

Becca's face lit up. "All *riiiight!*"

Now, only Nicky Pike is Becca's age, and he hates girls. Becca is friendly with a couple of his sisters, but not exactly best buddies.

So why was she so excited? I didn't know. But Becca was excited about a lot of things these days. Maybe she was going through a stage. And I guess the idea of a weekend afternoon without a playmate must have seemed pretty awful.

I did call Mr. and Mrs. Pike. They said they

were happy to have her over. And my parents agreed, too.

That was how I ended up walking to Mal's house with Becca the Jumping Bean.

She did not stop asking questions.

"When are your auditions for the Follies?"

"Monday, after school," I replied.

"*After school?* Can I watch?"

"Sorry, Becca. It's for sixth-graders only."

"Can you do that singer's voice again?"

"You mean Dolly Parton?"

"Yeah."

"Not in the street!"

"Please?"

By the time we got to the Pikes', I was singing "Nine to Five" in my best Dolly Parton voice.

Becca was cracking up. Neither of us noticed Nicky and Claire Pike at the side of the house.

But they noticed me.

"You stink," was Nicky's greeting to me.

I immediately stopped singing. "A-hem. Thank you."

Nicky is eight. He thinks everything stinks, except karate and whatever else boys at that age like.

Claire, on the other hand, is five. She thought I was great. "More! More!" she insisted.

Mr. Pike poked his head out the front door. "Hello, girls!"

"Hi!" Becca and I called out.

Crassshhh!

"Uh, excuse me." Mr. Pike ducked back into the house. A moment later I heard him yell, "Adam Pike! How many times have I told you not to climb on the kitchen counter?"

Thump-thump-thump-thump-thump! "What happened?"

That was Mrs. Pike, charging downstairs.

"I guess I'd better go in," I said to Becca.

I ran inside. Mr. Pike was picking up broken pieces of a bowl off the floor while Adam followed behind him with a Dust Buster and a sponge. A pool of milk was spreading, where a carton had fallen.

At the table, Jordan and Byron Pike were snickering at their brother. (Adam, Jordan, and Byron are ten-year-old triplets.)

Just beyond the kitchen, the back door swung open. Mallory flew inside, followed by two of her sisters, Vanessa (who's nine) and Margo (seven).

The three of them spoke at once:

"Hi, Jessi!" said Mal.

"Becca!" cried Vanessa.

"Adam, you are such a klutz!" exclaimed Margo.

Adam lunged at Margo with the Dust Buster. "Rrrraagghhh!"

"Stop!" Margo shouted. She stepped in the milk puddle and fell.

Jordan howled. "Who's the klutz?"

Mrs. Pike was leaning against the kitchen wall, shaking her head. "Welcome to the madhouse, Jessi," she said.

Needless to say, the Pike parents were gone within minutes (with relieved smiles on their faces). Mal and I prepared for the worst.

But the strangest thing happened. Becca took over. Yes, Becca, my little nuisance sister.

"Let's go outside," she suggested.

"Nahhh," Byron said. "I want to work on my model."

"Okay." Becca sighed. "Too bad you'll miss out on all the fun."

"What fun?" Byron looked skeptical.

"You won't know unless you come with us," Becca replied.

Mal and I followed them out. We took a couple of lounge chairs and put them in the sun. It was one of those perfect, cool days when the sun feels just right.

"Jessi," Mal said, "you have to read this new book. It is so cool . . ."

We gabbed and chatted, chatted and gabbed. I don't know how long it was before the revelation hit us.

We had actually had an entire conversation without one interruption.

Not one complaint. Not one injury. Nothing.

We looked over toward the garage. Becca and the Pikes were huddled in a rough circle, talking. Margo was laughing hysterically about something. Adam had that *boy* look — you know, that sneer that says, "I'm not interested at all. Tell me more!"

"What are they doing?" Mal asked.

"Let's move closer," I suggested.

We nonchalantly picked up our chairs and put them back down within earshot of the group.

Becca whispered something. All of them moved to the farthest corner of the yard.

Before long, Carolyn and Marilyn Arnold wandered by. (They're twins who live in the neighborhood.) "Hi!" Marilyn called out. "What're you doing?"

Becca waved them over. "Come on!"

Mal and I talked some more. When the kids all darted into the front yard, we shrugged and followed them.

We saw the triplets racing off down the street.

"Hey!" Mal called out. "Where are you going?"

"To the Barretts'!" Adam replied.

"Matt and Haley's!" Jordan and Byron called out. "To invite them over!"

Now, the triplets *are* ten, and those families are all in the neighborhood — but this was too sneaky for comfort.

"Thanks for asking," Mal snapped.

"Sorry," Adam shouted. "We'll be right back."

A few minutes later, the triplets returned, along with Buddy and Suzi Barrett, and Matt and Haley Braddock. Twelve kids altogether — ay-yi-yi!

But you know what? Becca had them enthralled. Mal and I had no idea what she was doing. When we were inside, they went out. When we were out, they went in.

We kept hearing giggles and laughs, though. And we didn't have to do a thing besides pour an occasional glass of apple juice.

It was the easiest sitting job I'd had in a long time. And I began wondering if the BSC would accept Becca as a *junior*-junior member.

A sitter-in-training, maybe? She could accompany me on all my jobs.

Mal laughed at the idea. She said the day was a total fluke. Next time they'd be at each other's throats.

Oh, well, it was worth a thought, wasn't it?

CHAPTER 7

When I walked to school Monday, there was a tennis ball in my throat.

Well, that was what it felt like. Big and scratchy and *stuck*.

"Hrrrr . . . hrrrr," I grunted.

"Jessi, we are approaching school," Claudia said. "Please behave yourself. If you toss a clam on the sidewalk while everyone's watching us, I swear I'll never speak to you again."

Mallory burst into giggles.

"A *clam*?" Stacey said with a grimace.

"Yes," Claudia replied. "She sounds like she's about to spit her guts out."

Thank goodness Mary Anne the Kind and Generous was with us. She said in a concerned voice, "Are you feeling all right, Jessi?"

"Fine," I said. "Just a little sore throat."

Strep. Mumps. Pneumonia. Those were the words that flew through my brain.

But I tried to block them out. Today was a

big day. First of all, I was going to help run auditions for the Follies.

Second of all, I was going to audition, myself.

I wished the two Dollies hadn't asked us committee members to try out for parts. I mean, they said it was just a formality — but *please*. What if I really blew it?

I knew I'd do well in the dancing department. But we each had to recite something from memory, like a poem or speech. And, worst of all, we had to *sing*.

Do you know what my singing voice sounds like? It peels wallpaper. It make dogs howl. It makes Jerry Lewis sound beautiful.

Okay, I'm going overboard. Once upon a time I thought I was a pretty good singer. But I'd learned the truth about my voice the hard way. Remember I told you about my triumph as the crocodile and the dog in *Peter Pan*? Well, I hadn't auditioned for those parts. I had tried out for the role of Peter. I was so sure I'd get it. Sigh.

Ever since then, I've been insecure about my singing. (I still think I might have gotten the part if only I could carry a tune better.)

And now it didn't help that on my big audition day a family of glop had decided to rent space in my throat.

"Hrrrrr . . . hrrrr. . . ."

We were entering the school now. Claudia rummaged in her purse and pulled out a paper packet. "Here, take one of these."

"What are they?"

"Special candy, guaranteed to clear your throat."

I ripped open the packet. It was filled with teeny black pellets. "How do they taste?" I dumped a few in my hand and popped them in my mouth.

Claudia's eyes grew about three sizes. "No! I said *one!*"

Too late. The troops had landed. I felt as if a small army with licorice-tipped sabers had invaded my mouth. My sinuses blew open. My eyes swelled with tears.

Mary Anne thrust a couple of tissues in front of me. I put them to my mouth and spat. "Augghhhh!"

"Are you okay?" Mallory asked.

"Yuck!" I gasped. "These are *horrible!*"

Claudia let out a low whistle of awe. "You won't have another sore throat until you're twenty-seven."

I ran to the nearest water fountain. It didn't help much. The cold water just irritated my throat. I didn't know if I'd ever talk again.

But at least the tennis ball was gone.

"I'm — I'm all right," I lied as I stood up from the fountain.

"Will you be able to sing for your audition?" Stacey asked.

"When I open my mouth I'll knock them out with the licorice smell," I replied. "They won't be able to hear a thing."

They laughed. We said our good-byes and headed for our lockers.

Sanjita was at hers, just closing up.

"Hi," I said. (Ooh, those *H* words tickled.)

She gave me a huge smile. "It's all set."

"What is?" I asked.

"You know. The toupee thing."

Duh, said my face.

Sanji sighed with exasperation. "Today's the day we're going to find out if Trout-Man is wearing a rug. Weren't you there when we planned it?"

I rememberd that Sanji and a few other kids had been gossiping after class last Monday, but I hadn't joined them.

"I guess not," I said.

Sanji giggled. "It's *perfect*. We're going to expose him in the middle of class."

"No! You wouldn't."

"Oh, come on, admit it, Jessi. You're dying to know about his hair."

"Well, yeah, but isn't this a little . . . mean?"

Sanji's smile disappeared. "Don't do anything to spoil this."

"But Sanji, how could they do something like that?"

"I'm not kidding."

I'd never seen Sanjita so serious. She was glaring at me.

"You know, I didn't have to tell you, Jessi. I trusted you."

What was the use? Class had already gotten so out of hand. If they didn't do this to Mr. Trout now, they'd just try it again some other time.

"Okay, okay," I said with a sigh.

I worried through homeroom. I worried through first and second period. I barely noticed the "good luck" note Mal passed me in class. If I wasn't thinking about the audition, I was thinking about the plot to de-hair Mr. Trout.

By Short Takes I was numb. It didn't help that every single person in class was on his or her best behavior.

Somehow, that was the creepiest thing of all.

People took notes and listened. Everyone was smiling. Mr. Trout must have thought he'd discovered the secret to Discipline by Doing Nothing. He actually tried to crack a joke or two, I think. (I don't know for sure.

With him, it was a little hard to tell.)

I had no idea what this plan was. Sanjita hadn't told me. I just sat, expecting the worst.

About halfway through the class, Mr. Trout began erasing the blackboard. "All right, I need a few volunteers to write a simpler version of the program we just did." He gestured toward the blackboard. "I'll add two points to your grade-point average if your program has the fewest steps."

Six kids jumped up from their desks. Mr. Trout's eyes practically popped out. Suddenly he looked completely different. I realized it was because I was seeing him smile for the first time.

"Uh, three at a time, please," he said.

Jimmy, Sandra, and John grumbled as they sat down. But they all had these sly little smiles I didn't trust.

Craig began writing on the left side of the board, Renee in the middle, and George on the right. Mr. Trout watched over their shoulders carefully.

His back, of course, was to the classroom.

After a couple of minutes, Mr. Trout stepped forward, to explain something to Renee. I noticed that Craig and George immediately stopped writing. Both were stepping back from the board, hands on chins, as if they were viewing their own work.

Craig stepped toward the corner, where a long, hooked wooden pole lay against the wall. He took the pole and tiptoed back.

I held my breath. Craig wouldn't do something really stupid, like *hit* Mr. Trout. Would he?

He raised the pole high and slipped the hooked end into the handle of a rolled-up world map directly above Mr. Trout. As Craig slowly pulled, the map rolled downward.

George was pulling something from his pocket that looked like a fish hook. When the map was in reach, he grabbed its handle and clipped the fish hook onto it.

Craig gently set down the pole, as George guided the other end of the fish hook into Mr. Trout's hair.

"So you see," Mr. Trout said to Renee, "those two steps may be combined — "

My heart stopped. He wasn't noticing a thing.

With a sharp flick of the wrist, George released the map. It slid upward into its metal tube with a *smack*.

Dangling from the hook was a limp patch of stiff, black fur.

The room fell silent. I caught a glimpse of shock on Craig's face. I closed my eyes. I couldn't bear to look at Mr. Trout.

Then the giggling started. It began with Maria and caught on.

When I opened my eyes, I saw the real Mr. Trout.

Wow, did he look different.

He had a ring of grayish-black hair that went up to the level of his ears. Above that, his scalp was as shiny as a pink mirror.

"Well." Mr. Trout was blushing. Above him, the toupee was bobbing around like a little lost animal. Craig, George, and Renee were gaping at it.

It was horrible. It was cruel. It was the worst prank I could possibly imagine.

But it was hilarious.

Maria was guffawing now. All around me, my classmates were red-faced with laughter. Someone called out "Conehead."

A laugh started out in my stomach, like a tickle. Then it began to spread through my body. I tried to keep it in, but I couldn't. It exploded out of me like a bomb. I was rocking in my seat, *sick* with laughter.

And then, just when I thought I was getting it under control, Mr. Trout began jumping up to try to grab his toupee. It seemed to be avoiding him, squirming out of the way. That just made everybody worse.

Finally he managed to grab it. "Well," he repeated, placing it back on his head. "Quite a humorous . . . interlude. You three may sit down."

As Craig, Renee, and George went back to their seats, Mr. Trout took an eraser and turned to the blackboard.

I collected myself. I reminded myself what a serious situation this was. I tried to think of it from Mr. Trout's point of view.

And then I caught a glimpse of something shiny on the back of the toupee.

It was the fish hook, swinging back and forth.

Forget it. The whole class was going, going, gone.

Well, news of the Balding of Mr. Trout spread through the school like wildfire. By the end of the day, everybody was talking about it.

My BSC friends wanted to hear every detail. They laughed at my description but agreed the trick was mean. Mary Anne was especially horrified. Kristy insisted that Mr. Trout "brought it on himself," and Stacey couldn't believe he didn't discipline anyone.

We gabbed so long, I almost forgot about my audition. Mal was the one who brought it up. By that time it was too late to be nervous.

Everyone wished me luck. Mal ran with me to the school. We hugged good-bye in front of the auditorium, and I dashed inside. I was determined to be fantastic!

CHAPTER 8

"Left, right, skip, skip! Arms up, jump . . . again!"

Again?

The gym was packed with sweating sixth-graders. Dolly One, in a skintight, neon-striped dance outfit, was leading all the auditioners in a dance combination.

The truth? It was more like an exercise class for the aerobically challenged.

March a little one way. March a little the other way. Hands up, hands down. Clap. Jump.

Ho-hum.

I knew a lot of the kids around me. In real life, they were perfectly well-coordinated. They could walk and talk at the same time. But here on the gym floor, they were transformed. It was as if their legs and arms had declared war on them.

I had never seen so many eleven-year-olds

fret about deciding left from right.

Okay, okay, I *know* it sounds snobby. But I was used to ballet class with Mme Noelle, who pitches a fit if your *demi-plié* is too *grande* for her taste.

(I don't even think she knows what the word "skip" means. She would be going crazy if she were here. "Skeep?" she would say. "What eez zees *skeep*? Zees ees not *donce!*")

But I skipped. And I reached. And I stepped. And when I got too bored I helped a couple of my friends.

When it was over, Dolly Two taught us a song.

I rememberd it from the video of last year's Follies. It was called "At SMS," and it was set to the tune of "Under the Sea" from *The Little Mermaid:*

At SMS the teachers cheer,
Because they won't have us next year.
We'll have it made
In seventh grade
At SMS. . . .

We all knew the tune, and the lyrics were funny. So it was pretty easy to learn.

But I wasn't exactly thrilled with the squawks that came from my mouth. I think Claudia's candies had made me even worse, if that were possible.

"All right, that sounds terrific!" Dolly Two

called out. "Now let's try putting together the song and the dance."

Half the group cheered. The other half looked petrified. Me? I fell in between.

The two Dollies started the music again. I leaped into the dance combination. And I sang at the top of my lungs.

Alone.

Well, that was what it felt like. All the loudest singers suddenly got laryngitis when they had to dance at the same time.

My voice echoed through the gym like a police siren. I was *mortified*. I thought the windows would crack.

I put my hand over my mouth and said, "Oops."

Dolly Two was smiling. "That was great, Jessi! Don't stop."

I tried. Honestly I did. But now I felt as if someone had put a twist-tie around my vocal cords. The police siren became a mouse squeak.

Very attractive.

It took a few run-throughs, but finally some other kids did start singing along.

"Okay, time for groups!" Dolly One called out. "We'll divide you into fours, so we can really see how you're doing. We'll be helping you out, so don't worry if it's not perfect."

She went through the gym, dividing us up.

Since about sixty people had shown up, that meant fifteen groups.

Mine was third. Nice and early.

I didn't make any mistakes. My voice didn't straighten out Dolly One's curls. I kept a smile on my face.

All in all, I was happy.

While the other groups danced, the rest of us waited in the stands. Us performance committee members sat near the Dollies' table. We had all helped set up the auditions — signing people in, alphabetizing names, stuff like that. But now nothing was left to do, except sit and get nervous about what came next.

I wanted so badly for Mal to be there — or *any* of my BSC friends — but the Dollies had decided on a "No Friends" rule. They thought too many people would make the auditioners nervous.

They were probably right, but I sure could have used some moral support.

After all the groups were finally finished, Dolly Two announced, "Now comes the hard part, kids — the individual audition. You will have a chance to sing a song *or* recite your memorized material."

Everyone just stared at her. We looked like the Zombies from Planet X.

"Look, this is not an audition for a Broadway show," Dolly Two said warmly. "Remember, you are all *in*. Every single one of you will be in the Follies. These tryouts are just to see where your strengths are, and where you need work. Sure, we'll select people to speak certain lines, sing a couple of solos — but more importantly, we need a good, big chorus. A chorus that looks like it's having fun. So just go out there and enjoy yourselves."

"Okay, we'll go alphabetically," Dolly One called out. "Ben Abbott!"

Ben raced onto the gym floor. He was so excited he nearly fell. He had nearly fallen during the dance combo, too. Fortunately he stayed upright during his speech. He delivered the Gettysburg Address, or something like it, at the top of his lungs:

"FORCE, GORE, AND SEVEN YEARS AGO OUR POOR FATHER BROUGHT FORTH ON THIS CONDIMENT A NEW NATION . . ."

The Dollies cut him off before we all cracked up (or lost our hearing).

Next Lauren Aronsen sang "Maybe" from the musical *Annie*. That was great.

Jeff Atkinson sang the theme song from *Shining Time Station*. He could have used a little more coal in his engine.

I heard everything from Shakespeare to sitcoms. A girl named Liz Cohen did the "Vitameatavegamin" routine from *I Love Lucy* (if you haven't seen that episode, you *must*). It was incredibly funny.

But *R* is pretty far into the alphabet. Which meant sitting through a lot of shy performers.

I thought I would turn into a fossil before my turn came. Fortunately I had my backpack, so I reached in and took out a book. I got so involved in it I didn't even hear Ms. Vandela call my name.

"Psssst! Go!"

A girl behind me tapped me on the shoulder.

"Me?" I said, bolting out of my seat.

The Dollies (and all the rest of the auditioners) were staring at me. "Come on down!" Ms. Vandela said.

Be a pro, Jessi, I said to myself.

I stood up straight. I smiled. I calmly walked onto the gym floor.

As I approached front and center, Ms. Bernhardt exclaimed, "Oh, good! You're doing something from *Maniac Magee*! I love that."

Huh?

I looked down. My right hand was still clutching the book I'd been reading.

"Oops. I was just . . . uh, wait a second . . ."

I ran back to the stands and gently tossed the book toward my backpack. It fell through the bleachers and slapped onto the floor.

So much for being a pro.

"Actually, I was going to recite 'The Owl and the Pussycat,' " I announced.

I'd recited that poem a million times to Squirt. I'd memorized it without even trying, then added some pantomime. Even Becca liked to watch me.

The minute I started, I knew I'd picked the wrong thing. In front of eleven-year-olds, I felt a little stupid.

But hey, I was a pro. I put all my energy into it.

The Dollies seemed to like it okay. But they started whispering to each other in the middle of it.

When I was done, Dolly One said, "Very nice reciting. Jessi, can you sing for us?"

"S-sing?"

Thook.

The tennis ball was back. It just popped up from my stomach and lodged in my throat.

"Sure," Dolly One said. "Anything. 'Happy Birthday,' even. If you don't mind. We just want to hear you."

Hadn't they heard enough of me during the group number? Did they want all the auditioners to go screaming for the exits?

I cleared my throat. My tennis ball was turning into a beach ball. My *Peter Pan* audition passed through my mind like an awful night-mare.

I knew one thing for sure. I was *not* going to sing "Happy Birthday."

"Uh, can I sing 'I Won't Grow Up' from *Peter Pan*?" (That was the song I *should* have sung at my other audition, instead of "I'm Flying.")

"Of course!" Ms. Bernhardt replied.

I swallowed and began:

"I'm never grow up, I'll won't grow up,
I don't want to go to tie —"

I stopped. A few kids were trying very hard not to giggle.

"Can I . . . start over?" I asked.

"Jessi, you sound fine," Dolly Two said. "Just relax and do it again."

I did. I made it through the song, and no one threw tomatoes at me.

I have no memory of the rest of the auditions. I was in a daze.

At the end, Dolly Two said, "Thank you all — and congratulations! You are the most talented sixth-graders I've seen! This is going to be the best show ever. We'll make all our casting decisions by Thursday, and they'll be posted in the main hall."

Everyone started gabbing excitedly. A couple of kids told me they thought I was great. I returned the compliments.

Then, with the rest of the committee members, I helped clean up. The Dollies were re-assuring to all of us. They teased me a little about "I Won't Grow Up" (Dolly Two said, "I'll really liked it!") but they made sure to say I had recovered beautifully.

After awhile, I started relaxing. I knew the show would be fun, no matter what part I landed.

I had to look on the bright side. I'd helped write the show, and I knew for a fact that not one part required a crocodile costume.

CHAPTER 9

I was flying.

My feet were off the ground. My brain was somewhere between the clouds and Neptune.

I, Jessica Ramsey, was going to play a Folly Dolly. But that's not the best part. At the bottom of Thursday morning's Follies list was this line:

(Assistant choreographer/dance captain: Jessica Ramsey.)

Now, I had *hinted* at the idea to the Dollies the week before — you know, "You guys could really use a dance captain to help you out, lah dee dah. . . ." That's all. I hadn't wanted to seem pushy, not after my *Peter Pan* experience.

But they had taken me seriously. Yea!

I was in the best mood all day. Even in Short Takes.

Are you wondering what happened to Mr. Trout? Well, he went back to wearing his toupee. True to his style, he never said a thing about what had happened.

Since the Great Balding, the class had settled down. Well, sort of. What I mean is, the creativity level of the pranks had peaked. Now it was all downhill. Kids were back to spitballs and note-passing and the usual dumb stuff.

So when a note was slipped onto my desk, I wasn't too surprised. I figured it was another "Drop Your Books" command or something.

I opened it up and read:

Dear Jessi,
Please meet me in
the hallway after class.
Important!!!!
Jus

I looked over at Justine Moss. She gave me a shy smile.

Justine is about the last person in the world I'd have expected a note from. She's quiet and studious. But she was on the performance committee, so I figured she had some Follies news.

I waited outside the room after class.

78

"Come with me," Justine said as she stepped through the door.

I followed her around the corner. She stopped in front of some lockers.

"What's up?" I asked.

She looked like she was about to burst. "I had the greatest idea this morning."

"What?"

"You know that skit we couldn't figure out how to end — the one where all the celebrities start arguing in the teachers' lounge."

"Uh-huh."

"Well, how about this. Just when things start to get bad, in walks Mr. Williams as Elvis. And everyone says, 'I thought you died!' And he says, 'Ah didn't dah, ah wuz kidnapped by Klingons!' You know what a Klingon is, from *Star Trek*?"

"Those ugly bald guys, right?"

"Right. And in walks one with a phaser — and it's Mr. Trout!"

"Uh-huh. Well, I don't know . . ."

"Played by *you*, Jessi — in a bald wig!"

"Whoa. Hang on, Jus. I don't mind playing a Folly Dolly, but — "

"It's the same thing, Jessi!" Justine insisted.

"No, it's not."

Justine folded her arms. "I already told the Dollies, and they thought it was a great idea. Besides, look what we have already. One person is playing Mr. Williams with a pot belly. You're doing a Folly Dolly with a wig and a stuffed blouse. . . ."

She went on and on. One of our teachers, Mr. Jazak, wears Coke-bottle glasses — and we had written a part for someone with plastic Coke bottles sticking out of his glasses. One sixth-grader was going to portray our woodshop teacher like Pigpen from "Peanuts," only with sawdust falling wherever he goes, instead of dirt. Another kid was going to play our music teacher, Mrs. Pinelli, bursting into song with a terrible operatic voice every time she spoke. Stuff like that.

"I guess we're really going overboard, huh?" I said.

"Going overboard is the whole point, Jessi. Remember last year's video, when it showed the audience? The teachers were hysterical!"

"Do you think *Mr. Trout* will laugh at himself?" I asked.

Justine sighed. "Look, I don't like it when everyone's mean to him, either. But the Follies is the opposite of mean. It's showing the teachers how much we like them. It's like saying, 'You're one of us.' And the toupee isn't a *secret* or anything. Everybody knows about it now. Besides, I already mentioned the idea to Ms. Bernhardt, and you know what *she* said? 'You guys are so sweet to include him!' "

Rrriiinnnng!

"Oops!" I started to run to my fourth-period class. "We'll talk later!"

"Think about it!" Justine yelled.

"I will!"

I did, too. But I still wasn't convinced. In fact, when I went to the rehearsal after school, I was all ready to tell Justine I'd decided against it.

"Okay, places for the *Wayne's World* number!" Dolly One announced the moment I walked in.

I quickly sat down to watch. Bobby Gustavson and another boy played Wayne and Garth in an SMS class, giving idiotic answers and making total chaos. Jamie Sperling played the teacher, Ms. Flood, who speaks in an Australian accent. She kept calling Bobby "Woin."

Then, when the entire cast had arrived, Ms. Bernhardt put us all through our big production number — and she let me help out with the choreography.

Next we split into two groups. Ms. Bernhardt went off to the back of the auditorium to work on some smaller skits, while Ms. Vandela directed the teachers' lounge skit onstage. First she described Justine's idea to everybody, then commanded, "Okay, Elvis and Klingon in the wings. The rest of you, places!"

"Uh, Ms. Vandela?" I called out.

I was all set to tell her my decision about not playing Mr. Trout, but another student was already bending her ear about something.

I climbed onstage. Randy Rademacher, who was playing Mr. Williams/Elvis, grinned at me. He was wearing his '50s shades and was combing his hair back. "Wuzz up, Trout-Man?" he asked in his Elvis voice.

Justine ran up to me, holding a floppy brown piece of Latex. "Here, try this on."

"Uh, well — " I began.

Randy burst into hysterical laughter. "Check it out! A bald cap!"

Now everybody was looking at me. I held out the limp cap to Justine. "Sorry, I can't — "

"Come on . . ." Justine urged.

"Let's see! Let's see!" Randy said.

"It's just a joke!" someone yelled from onstage.

Mara Semple was in the skit, too — Mara, the girl who wasn't allowed to visit my house. I could see her rolling her eyes and mumbling to the girl next to her.

Ms. Vandela was now looking at us curiously. "Is something wrong?"

I took a deep breath. Here's what went through my mind:

It was *one* imitation.

It wasn't the worst.

It wasn't the longest.

If Mr. Trout could take the Balding without losing his temper, he wouldn't mind this — especially if *all* the other teachers were laughing at their own imitations.

I didn't want to blow it. It had taken me a long time to feel *accepted* at SMS. Everybody seemed to respect my talents. They wanted *me* to play Mr. Trout, even though I was the wrong sex and skin color.

Besides, if I chickened out, the Mara Semple types would not let me forget it.

That's show biz, I said to myself.

I stretched out the latex cap and put it on my head. In my usual ballerina style, my hair was pulled straight back, flat against my scalp. The wig snapped right into place.

"Uh, now then," I said in a nasal Trout voice. "Has anyone seen my, uh, hair?"

The whole auditorium went up. *Roared.* Even Mara was cackling.

You know what? It felt great.

Then Randy started singing, "You ain't nothin' but a Chrome Dome, shinin' all the time!"

"Is someone writing this down?" Ms. Bernhardt called out.

Two kids grabbed their clipboards.

Randy and I were hot. We went on improvising for a few minutes. Ms. Vandela was weeping with laughter.

We had practically a whole new skit — and the last thing Ms. Vandela said before we all went home was, "You guys are going to steal the show."

Afterward, the finance committee all walked to my house for its final meeting. The whole way, we could not stop talking about the skit.

The rehearsal had run late, and Mama and Daddy insisted on feeding the entire committee dinner. At the table, we told everyone about the Elvis/Klingon routine.

Then I put on the bald wig. Well, I thought Becca was going to have a heart attack. I have never heard that girl laugh so hard.

When dinner was over, the committee went into the living room and compared notes. Each of us had called possible organizations and asked for information. Many of the groups had sent brochures.

We talked about them all. We passed some of the materials around. We discussed the causes we liked the most.

And guess what? At the end of the meeting, I proudly printed on the draft of our official program, "The proceeds from the Sixth-Grade Follies will be donated to the Stamford Theater for the Hearing-Impaired."

All in all, it had been a great day.

Wednesday

Follies, Follies, Follies. The world
is gripped with Follies Fever. Was
it _this_ exciting two years ago?
   Maybe, but I don't think so.
Anyway, I certainly didn't expect
the Follies to hold the key to the
Mystery of the Baby-sitters Club....

That's Baby-sit*tees* Club, as opposed to Baby-sit*ters* Club. Stacey made that up. The sittees she was talking about were Becca, Charlotte, Haley, Vanessa, and Margo. And the reason for Follies Fever was that *the Sixth-Grade Follies were only two days away!* Between rehearsals, baby-sitting, and ballet classes, the days had whooshed by.

Aghhhhh! I was totally psyched. Rehearsals had been going great, and I had perfected my Mr. Trout voice. I was even using the voice in BSC meetings, which drove everybody crazy.

But more about that later. Back to Stacey and the Great Mystery.

Actually, she was only supposed to sit for Charlotte that afternoon. It was pouring outside, so Stacey made sure to bring along her Kid-Kit full of puzzle books, games, and art supplies.

"Anybody home?" Stacey called through the back screen door of the Johanssen house.

"Stacey, come in!" Dr. Johanssen said, rushing to open the door. "I'll take your wet stuff."

As Dr. Johanssen bustled away with Stacey's raincoat, Charlotte came into the kitchen (which is just off the back entrance).

"Hi, Stacey," she said.

"Hi!" Stacey replied. "What a day, huh?"

"It stinks. I wish it didn't have to rain."

"Well, I brought a brand-new book of word games."

"Uh-huh."

"And Mad Libs, and a new set of markers."

"Good."

" 'Bye, girls!" Mr. Johanssen called out as he and his wife flew by. They were on their way to an important town meeting. "There's plenty of snack stuff in the fridge."

Charlotte followed them to the front door. She kept looking out the window after they left.

And looking.

"Charlotte, are you okay?" Stacey asked.

"Yeah. Perfect."

Something was up. Charlotte was hardly ever this quiet and distracted. And no one knows Charlotte better than Stacey. The two of them call each other "almost sisters." Everyone says that Char used to be painfully shy until Stacey brought her out of her shell.

"Well," Stacey said in her most cheerful voice, "I think Mad Libs are perfect for a rainy day."

But just as Stacey reached into the Kid-Kit, Charlotte ran to the door. "Hi!" she screamed as she pulled it open.

"Hi!" squealed two voices.

Stacey looked out the window to see Margo

and Vanessa running across the soggy lawn. The Pikes' station wagon was pulling out of the driveway.

"I didn't know you were having visitors," Stacey said.

"Well, I am," Charlotte replied with a big smile.

"Uh, do your parents know?"

"Hm. I guess I forgot to tell them. Please, Stacey. Please can they stay?"

"Please please please please please!" Margo squealed.

"Sure."

Now, Stacey didn't *mind* the extra kids, of course. But the secrecy was a little odd, especially from Charlotte.

It was even odder when Haley Braddock appeared at the front door in her rain slicker.

And a few minutes later, Becca Ramsey.

Yes, my family was involved in this, too. Becca had told my parents that Char had invited her, and that it was all right with the Johanssens.

Either Charlotte or Becca was being a little sneak.

Needless to say, the Mad Libs stayed in the Kid-Kit.

"We're going into the rec room, okay?" Char said to Stacey.

"Okay."

Stacey followed them, but when Char got to the door, she announced, "Kids only. This is top secret."

"No problem."

Cool. Stacey knows kids. They love stuff like that.

She went into the living room and found some magazines to read.

After a *Vogue*, a *New York*, a *Ranger Rick*, and a stab at *Journal of the American Medical Association* (zzzzz), Stacey's mind started to wander.

Giggles were wafting in from the rec room.

And music, from a tape recorder.

And singing.

Hmmm.

Stacey put down the magazine and wandered closer to the rec room. She heard Vanessa singing the *Sesame Street* song, ending with the words, "Won't you smell my Sesame Feet?"

"Eewww!" the others screamed, giggling like crazy.

Okay. Silly songs. Maybe they were embarrassed. That's why they didn't want Stacey to hear.

Back to the living room. A little homework, a cup of tea, listening to children's laughter and raindrops. What an easy job. La-dee-dah.

All of a sudden, Haley came running in, all excited.

"Stacey, is Kristy the president of the Baby-sitters Club?" she asked.

"Uh-huh."

"And what are you?"

"Treasurer."

"And Claudia's vice-president?"

"Right. Haley, why do you want to know this stuff?"

"Um, we were arguing about it, that's all."

"Oh."

Exit.

More screaming and laughing. Louder music. Stacey was going nuts. She could not concentrate.

Then, suddenly, the noise stopped.

A minute later, all five girls came barrelling into the room. "Were we too loud?" Charlotte asked.

"Well . . . no," Stacey lied.

Haley looked worried. "Did you hear what we were saying?"

"No."

"Oh, good," Charlotte said. "We're going to work on something else now. Something quiet."

"But it's still secret," Margo warned.

"Fine," Stacey said.

The girls bolted from the living room. They ran frantically around the house, giggling. Stacey could hear drawers opening and closing. Through the living room archway she saw Charlotte heading toward the rec room with glue and scissors.

"Don't come in until we say it's okay!" Vanessa shouted from inside.

"I won't!" Stacey answered.

Well, she waited. And waited. Stacey finished her homework. She could hear occasional rips, snips, and giggles.

At 5:15 she began packing up. Mr. and Dr. Johanssen were due back and Stacey had to go to a BSC meeting.

At 5:17 the Johanssens arrived. Stacey explained about Charlotte's visitors.

At 5:19, when Stacey was heading for the door, the girls came barging into the living room.

"Wait!" Charlotte said. "Take this with you!"

She handed Stacey a huge, handmade envelope that looked like this:

"Whoa. What's this?" Stacey asked.

"It's for the whole Baby-sitters Club," Charlotte explained.

"But don't open it until *everybody's* there," Vanessa insisted. "It's *important*."

For about the hundredth time, Stacey nodded seriously and said, "Okay."

Stacey couldn't wait to open it. But she did exactly what the kids had wanted.

As it turned out, Stacey was the last to arrive at the meeting. "Order!" Kristy boomed as Stacey walked through the door.

"Burger, medium rare!" Logan Bruno replied. (He *always* says stuff like that when he comes to meetings.)

"Not funny anymore, Bruno," Kristy muttered.

"Maybe you should say something else to open meetings, Kristy," Claudia suggested. "Like . . . I don't know, 'Yabba dabba doo!' "

Everybody laughed. "It's five-thirty," Kristy shouted. *"Yabba dabba doo! I like it!"*

"Wilmaaaaaa!" Logan bellowed in a horrible Fred Flintstone imitation.

"Okay, enough!" President Kristy snapped. "Any new business?"

Stacey held out the letter. "This is for us, from Charlotte and her friends."

She showed it around. Everyone leaned forward. "Open it," Mary Anne urged.

Stacey ripped it open and read it aloud:

Privat invitation !!!
Come one come all
to THE WORLD FAMOUS
BSc FOLLYS !!!!!
One day only !!
A week from Saturday!!!
AT CHARLOTTES' HOUSE
Rsvp Write away
555- 8479

"The BSC Follies?" Shannon said.

"That is sooo cute!" Mary Anne exclaimed.

I laughed. No wonder Becca had been so interested in finding out about the Follies! (I learned later that she'd thought of the idea.)

"Can I call them?" Stacey asked.

"Sure," Claud said, handing her the phone.

Stacey tapped out Charlotte's number. "Hi, Char, it's your almost sister . . . uh-huh. . . . We loved it! And *we accept!*"

CHAPTER 11

"*She's here! Line up for the finale!*" Ms. Bernhardt bellowed.

Those were the first words I heard as I raced into the auditorium.

Or, I should say, the first words I could make out.

Everything else was a jumble — screaming, line practicing, laughter, arguing.

It was magic time!

Well, magic time minus one hour.

Friday had arrived at last. Me? I was a basket case. For days, my mind had been on nothing but the Follies. In ballet class that week, Mme Noelle said my mind was "in zee ozone."

That evening I could barely touch dinner. My stomach growled as I walked into the auditorium, but all I could think was: *Did I bring my bald head? Did I bring my dance shoes? What comes after chassé left?*

I was also singing, "Yoo-ee you-ee you-ee

94

you-ee you-ee," up and down a scale. That's something Shannon taught me. It's called a vocalise, and it's pronounced *vocal-ease* — but it should be called vocal-*hard*, because your lips start to hurt after doing it too much. (Why "you-ee" as opposed to "Me-you," or "P.U.," or "yabba-dabba-doo"? Don't ask me.) Anyway, it's supposed to make you sing better.

Am I making sense? I hope so, because I still get all worked up just thinking about that day.

"Jessi?"

I became aware of Ms. Vandela's voice in the middle of a "you" on the way to an "ee."

"Huh?" I said.

"Uh, the kids are lining up for the dance finale. I'd like one run-through while we have time. Will you lead them?"

"Yes."

It was a good idea. We'd had a dress rehearsal for the finale the day before, and it had been, well, interesting.

Oh, okay, the truth. It had been *horrible*.

The entire cast was in the finale. And I mean everyone, including kids whose feet seem to grow roots at the sound of the word "dance."

Now don't get me wrong. This "dance" was not like something at the American Ballet Theatre. Just some loose, hip-hop stuff, followed by a kickline. Simple. Fun.

Here's what happened at the dress rehearsal: Ben Abbott, who had worn his Top-Siders, flung them both into the seats during the kickline. Sarah Green had gotten so nervous she had to take a barf break in the girls' room. And Ashley Bedell had stormed offstage, saying the routine was too hard.

Well, Ben, Sarah, and Ashley were all there on Friday, raring to go. (And Ben was wearing tightly tied running shoes.)

Dolly Two, who was our piano accompanist, looked at me patiently. "Okay, places for the finale!" I shouted.

Everybody scrambled into place. Dolly Two began the intro. I counted out the correct number of beats, then shouted, "Three and four and *go!*"

Oh, boy.

Ben looked like he was trying to kick a field goal. A couple of the other guys seemed to be involved in Ninja training. And two of the girls ended up dancing right off into the backstage area.

"Hold it!" I called out. "Stop the music."

I was no longer nervous. It was time for some serious action. I hopped onstage and demonstrated. I answered questions. I simplified steps.

The second attempt was much better. I watched it sitting next to Ms. Vandela on the piano. "Let me do one more run-through," I said.

"That's all the time we have, I'm afraid," she said to me gently. "We have to get ready."

I looked at her. She looked at me.

"Eeeee!" we both screamed, hugging each other.

I love the Dollies. They are just like two kids.

"Okay, everybody gather round!" Ms. Bernhardt called out.

We all came to the front of the stage. The Dollies told us how wonderful we'd been. They said this was the best show they'd ever worked on. And . . .

They were going to treat us to ice cream in the cafeteria after the show!

"Yea!" everyone yelled.

Then we went to work. The light crew turned the lights on and off a million times. The sound crew kept repeating "Testing" over and over, even though we only had two mikes. The costume crew scrambled around backstage with needles, thread, and measuring tape.

I went back into the hallway. There, under the bright lights, the makeup people were busy fussing with everyone's faces.

"Jessi?"

I turned to see Mallory waving to me. She was at the end of the hallway, near the lobby.

I ran to her. We practically smothered each other with hugs.

"Break a leg!" she said.

"Thanks!" I replied. "Ohhhh, I wish you were in this!"

"No way! I'm going to lead your cheering section!"

We hugged again and I ran back to the makeup table.

I sat next to Jamie Sperling, who was struggling with her blonde wig. She and I were to open the show as the Folly Dollies. (Our wigs were on loan from the high school costume shop.)

I pulled my wig over my head. It fit fine. Then I slathered on the makeup.

Kids were zooming back and forth. A girl carrying light bulbs almost collided with a guy carrying props. Ben was practicing the steps for the finale. Three girls were singing the words, to help him out.

It was an absolute, total zoo.

"How do ah look?" Jamie said, standing up in her full Dolly getup.

"Beautiful," I replied. "And me?"

"Well . . ."

We looked soooo stupid. It was hilarious.

The hallway clock said 7:35. Twenty-five minutes to go. I had to see the audience.

I ran backstage. The noise of the crowd was

coming through the curtain, all muffled. I sneaked stage right and took a peak, pulling the curtain aside.

The Pikes were negotiating their seats, making a whole row of people move over. Kristy and her family were sitting right behind them. Claudia was in the back of the auditorium, gabbing with Mary Anne and Logan.

So many people were filing in. The auditorium was almost half full. In just a little while the lights would dim, and we'd be on our way.

I started to shiver. This was nothing like a ballet performance. No routines, no music to guide me along. Just me, Jamie, and the audience. If we did well, they'd laugh. If not . . . well, I didn't want to think about that.

"Pssssst! Jessi!"

I looked down at the front row. Becca was waving to me, grinning from ear to ear. I could tell Mama was trying not to screech with laughter at my outfit.

Daddy didn't see me. He was helping Aunt Cecelia with her coat. She, of course, looked exasperated.

Then, out of the corner of my eye, I saw *him*.

Mr. Trout.

He was walking into the auditorium, alone. His toupee was shiny in the glare of the house lights. He took a seat way in the back, opened up a paperback, and started reading.

Suddenly my stomach felt like a pinball machine. I let the curtain fall in front of me.

All my doubts came rushing back into my brain.

What was I doing?

But I had no time to think about it. The two Dollies were rampaging around in their high heels, yelling, "Clear the stage! Fifteen minutes!"

"Full house, kids!" someone yelled from behind me. "The ticket people say we're sold out!"

The whole cast cheered like crazy.

Sold out! I was thrilled. That meant a nice, big check to the Theater for the Deaf.

I went back into the hallway, where everybody was still hugging and doing last-minute practicing.

Ms. Bernhardt called "Ten minutes."

Then "Five."

Then "Places."

Jamie and I met at center stage. We were too nervous to hug. Finally Ms. Bernhardt yelled, "Curtain up!"

Nothing happened.

"Pull it the other way!" Ms. Bernhardt hissed.

"Oh." The boy pulling the curtain yanked again. The two halves of the curtain parted.

Jamie and I faced total darkness. I got ready to speak.

But I couldn't say a word. The audience started *howling* — at our costumes!

I stalled for time, fluffing my hair.

They howled again.

When I finally got around to saying my first line: "Gee, Ms. Vandela, do you think we have enough talent in this school to have a Follies?" the whole audience answered, *"Yes!"*

We were off and running.

In the Folly Dollies introduction, we pretended it would be too hard to find enough kids who could sing and dance to put on a show.

In the next skit, Dolly Two (Jamie) went into a gym class, and all the kids burst into a rap song. The *Wayne's World* skit followed right after that.

The teachers' lounge skit came pretty late in the show. I froze up a little, thinking about Mr. Trout, there in the audience. As I waited for my cue line backstage, I almost chickened out.

But then I heard Bobby say, "Ah'm not dead. Ah wuz kidnapped by Mr. Trout, the Klingon."

I stepped out, bald wig and all, and said, "*Kwing*on. Pwease."

Well, I thought I was going to have to stay

there all night. The laughter went on forever. I could not keep a straight face. All the kids on stage were cracking up.

I don't know how we got through the number.

We did, though. Somehow. And before I knew it, the finale had snuck up on us.

I held my breath. We all lined up onstage, arms around each other's shoulders. To my right was Mara Semple. She gave me a squeeze.

When I looked at her, she was beaming. "You are so talented," she said.

Then the curtain opened. And I danced my heart out. I didn't care if it was too easy, or not really *"donce."* To me, it was just as important as any ballet.

And you know what? Ben was fabulous. So were Sarah and Ashley. When we got to the kickline, the audience was on its feet, clapping in rhythm. We couldn't even hear the piano.

Everyone kept standing, right through the curtain call. The grown-ups were cheering and saying "Bravo!" I could hear loud screaming from the Pikes' row. Plus a loud whistle, followed by, "Yo, Jessi!" which could only have been Kristy.

I was smiling so hard I thought my face would get stuck.

Afterward we all raced into the hallway. It

was a huge hugfest. I must have said "You were great!" seven hundred times — and I meant every one.

The two Dollies told Jamie and me we were so good, they wanted us to take over their classes.

I saw Mr. Williams and Bobby doing an Elvis *duo*.

Mrs. Pinelli, our music teacher with the operatic voice, was laughing so much she was *hooting*.

The teachers were such good sports. They really seemed delighted by our imitations. I looked around for Mr. Trout, but it was so crowded I couldn't tell if he'd come backstage.

"Jessi Jessi Jessi Jessi!"

Becca practically tackled me. Behind her, Mama and Daddy were beaming. "Did you like it?" I asked.

"You were a star," Daddy said.

"I almost fell out of my seat," Mama added.

Even Aunt Cecelia had something nice to say. "I was proud of my niece — except one of your teachers would not stop slapping the armrest next to me. Now, funny is funny, but he could have been a little more courteous to his neighbors!"

Leave it to Aunt Cecelia.

"Who wants ice cream?" I asked.

"Me!" Becca screamed.

We all made our way to the cafeteria. The entire BSC was waiting there. Every single one of them mobbed me.

Except one.

Claudia was mobbing the ice cream.

CHAPTER 12

Boy, did I sleep well Friday night.

I woke up Saturday to the ringing of the phone. It was Jamie. We had a screaming-for-happiness contest.

Then Justine called. And Randy. And Bobby. And, of course, Mallory.

After Mal's call, I went to the kitchen and yakked with my family. Mama said she hadn't known I had such a "sense of comedy." Daddy repeated his favorite parts of the show, doing imitations of *our* imitations. Becca looked at me all starry-eyed. And Aunt Cecelia came in and complained about her feet.

(Actually she did manage a compliment or two.)

"Who's hungry?" Daddy boomed.

"Me!" we all replied.

He made us a humongous breakfast of eggs, bacon, and toasted bagels. I ate every last crumb. I was *starving*. (I don't know why. I had stuffed myself with praline fudge ice cream the night before.)

The nicest part of that morning was a call from Ms. Bernhardt. When she told me how much money the Follies had raised, I almost fainted.

"I'd like three students to come with me to Stamford to present the check on Monday," she said. "And I want you to be one of them. After all, the organization was your suggestion."

Wasn't that nice of her? My parents agreed right away.

I don't know where the rest of the weekend went. I do know that I spent most of it going over every second of the show in my head.

From time to time I thought about Mr. Trout. No one had mentioned a word about him after the show or over the phone. I hoped he had enjoyed himself.

He must have. Every other teacher loved the show. Even if you didn't have much of a sense of humor, you couldn't help laughing that night.

I was sure the atmosphere had rubbed off.

Still, I was nervous as I walked to school with Mal on Monday.

The sixth-graders, I must admit, were the

center of attention in the main hallway. Jamie was surrounded by kids who were jabbering about the show. Ms. Bernhardt was trying to cross to the administration office, but everyone was stopping her to talk.

"Jessi!"

Jamie rushed up to me. Before long, we were joined by Justine, Bobby, and Sanjita.

Yes, Sanji had been at the show, too. And she *adored* the Mr. Trout imitation. (Surprised?)

I think we would have chatted away the whole day if the homeroom bell hadn't rung.

I saw Sanjita again just after first period. She had that Juicy Gossip look in her eye.

"Jessi, did you hear what happened?" she asked.

"No," I replied.

"Trout's out."

"Huh?"

"He hasn't come to school today. I heard Mr. Kingbridge talking about him with Mrs. Downey. They don't know where he is. He didn't even call to arrange a sub."

My stomach sank. "Uh-oh."

"He couldn't even stick out the last week of Short Takes." Sanji giggled. "You really did it, Jessi."

"Yeah. I guess."

"You ought to be on *Saturday Night Live*. See you!"

Now, Sanjita had meant all that as a compliment (I think). But I felt as if I'd been hit by a truck.

Mr. Kingbridge is our assistant principal and Mrs. Downey our school secretary. If they said Mr. Trout wasn't here, it had to be true.

I had driven him away. I had hurt him so badly he couldn't even call the school.

On my way to second period, I started to cry.

I was a mess in class. I couldn't think about anything else. Afterward, Mal tried to cheer me up, but that was impossible.

Between second and third periods, the whole school seemed to be talking about Mr. Trout.

I heard someone say my skit had been the last straw. Mr. Trout had been fuming underneath, and he finally broke.

Someone else said he had resigned.

Moved out of town.

Left the state.

Left the country.

Threw his toupee in a river and became a monk.

I didn't find any of this funny. Especially the way some kids were treating me. Their conversations would drop to a whisper as I passed by.

I was petrified of going to Short Takes. What if all the rumors were untrue? What if he was just late? What would I say when he walked into class?

Well, as it turned out, I didn't have to worry on that score, at least. A substitute was waiting for us.

For some reason, the first thing I noticed was his hair. Definitely real. Grayish-brown, thinning on top. He was a little overweight and wore glasses and a blue blazer. He looked sort of . . . average.

You know what it's like when a sub shows up. So you can imagine what my Short Takes class was like. They were *already* used to pranks and wisecracks.

Now it looked like April Fool's Day.

"Hey, Kwingon!" Craig Avazian yelled as I entered.

"Yea, Jessi!" Janet O'Neal cheered. "Great job!"

John Rosen let out a whistle. A couple other kids applauded. Maria Fazio said, "Mr. Twout wan away!" and burst out laughing at her own joke.

"All *right!*"

A deep voice echoed through the room like a gunshot.

The sub stood up, holding the seating chart in front of him. "Obviously you are not following this plan. So I would like you all to move." Grumbling, everyone got up and arranged themselves according to the chart. Then the sub said, "Okay. Mr. Rosen, Ms. Fazio, Mr. Avazian, Ms. O'Neal. This is Warning One. I give *only* one. Is that understood?"

Silence.

"Now, my name is Mr. Bellafatto, and I — "

Maria exploded with giggles. *"Bellafatto?"* she repeated under her breath.

The sub stopped speaking. He looked at her calmly and said, "I will be here tomorrow and the remainder of the week. I give homework assignments. And you, young woman, will have twice as much as the rest of the class."

"But — but I — " Maria sputtered.

Mr. Bellafatto picked up some chalk and turned to the blackboard. "Now, I'm here on short notice, but I have an idea what you've been learning, so I'll try to fumble my way through — "

While his back was turned, a huge glob of spitball went flying through the air. It landed with a *splat* in Renee Johnson's hair.

"Ewwwww! Mr. Bella — "

"Good shot," Mr. Bellafatto said to Craig (I don't know *how* he could have seen him).

Craig squirmed. He laughed nervously.

"So good, in fact, I think you should let the principal know how talented you are. Right now."

Craig's jaw hit the ground. "But — but I — "

"Hmm. You and Ms. Fazio ought to get together. You have the same vocabulary — 'but, but, but.' Do you know the way to the office, or must I send an escort?"

Craig meekly stood up. His lower lip was quivering as he left the room.

Everyone sat forward.

Whoa. This guy was amazing.

What a difference.

With a smile, he said, "You'll find I'm actually not a bad guy . . . for a teacher." He shrugged. "All I ask is that you show a little courtesy. Are you all right, Ms. . . . ah . . ." He checked the seating plan again. "Johnson?"

Renee nodded quickly. "Uh-huh."

"Good. Let's get started."

He didn't exactly pick up where Mr. Trout had left off. I think he went back to an earlier stage of the curriculum. It was hard to tell.

But it didn't matter. After a few minutes, I realized that I actually understood what he was talking about. *That* was a change. For a sub, he was a pretty good teacher. He explained things clearly, answered questions, and he even cracked a few jokes.

And I wasn't distracted by pranks and notes and whispers. They had stopped. Completely.

When he didn't have to discipline anyone, Mr. Bellafatto was basically a funny, normal guy.

By the end of class, I could sense this *relief* in the air.

It should have felt great. I should have been happy that I was finally understanding computer gobbledygook.

But I wasn't. All I could think about was how I had destroyed poor Mr. Trout.

After school I met the two Dollies in front of the school, along with Lisa Mannheim and Tom Block, two other kids on the Finance Committee.

Ms. Bernhardt drove us all to Stamford. In the car, I tried to gush about the show with everyone else. When Tom mentioned the Mr. Trout skit, I just smiled and nodded. I didn't want to talk about it at all.

But everyone else did. At one point Lisa asked the two Dollies, "Has anyone heard from him?"

Ms. Vandela sighed. "Mr. Kingbridge was talking to him on the phone as we were leaving. He didn't sound too happy."

Oh, boy.

When we arrived at the theater office, the

manager and director were delighted to see us. The two Dollies insisted that I present the check.

I did. And I have never felt so proud and so rotten at the same time.

CHAPTER 13

I t wasn't just me.

That's what I had decided by Wednesday morning. I had thought about it a million times.

I was not the only cause of Mr. Trout's troubles. Craig was and Maria was and the whole class was. Of course he had left. Who could have put up with all of that?

But even though I wasn't *totally* to blame, my skit had put him over the edge. So I felt I had to do something.

Before school, I spotted Ms. Bernhardt near my locker. "Hi," I said.

"Jessica! How's the star?"

I shrugged. "Okay, I guess. Um, I was wondering if you'd heard anything about Mr. Trout?"

Ms. Bernhardt exhaled and shook her head. "Oh, that *man*. He gave Mr. Kingbridge such a hard time."

"Really?"

"Well, he didn't give any warning — *nothing*. Just didn't show up. Mr. Kingbridge tried calling him Monday morning, but his phone was disconnected. Do you know what it's like to get a sub on two hours' notice — when you're not even sure if the teacher is officially absent? Goodness, after awhile Mr. Kingbridge thought something terrible might have happened, so he spent lunch period *driving* to Mr. Trout's house. Nobody was home. No car in the driveway."

"Wait," I said. "If his phone was disconnected, how could Mr. Kingbridge have been talking with him when we all left for Stamford after school Monday?"

"Mr. Trout called him from a pay phone," Ms. Bernhardt replied. "He was at a gas station somewhere in Vermont. He'd decided he couldn't take it anymore. Can you believe that? *Vermont!*"

My eyes started welling up again. "So it *was* the Follies!"

"Sweetheart, if it wasn't that it would have been something else. Honestly, that fellow sure needed to lighten up a bit. I never so much as got a 'Good morning' out of him — none of us teachers did. Are we so . . . so *unapproachable*?"

I couldn't speak. Ms. Bernhardt could see I

was upset, and she put her arm around me. "Hey, don't blame yourself. You didn't do anything wrong. If anybody should have been insulted, it should have been *me*! That wig of yours looked like a rat's nest!"

I couldn't help giggling. Ms. Bernhardt gave me a squeeze. "Don't worry," was the last thing she said before heading off to her class.

By the third period bell, Mr. Bellafatto hadn't arrived for Short Takes. He walked in a few minutes late, with Mr. Kingbridge.

"Uh, kids, I have an announcement to make," Mr. Kingbridge said. "Your regular teacher, Mr. Trout, has decided to . . . well, to take an unexpected leave of absence. He's . . . ah, contemplating going back to graduate school, I believe. For the brief duration of this Short Takes segment, Mr. Bellafatto will be your official teacher. Please make him feel welcome."

"Yea!" cheered a few students.

Mr. Bellafatto took a modest bow.

I couldn't stand it anymore. Mr. Trout had been here, had gone through such torment, and now — *poof!* — just like that, everyone was going to forget him.

Well, not me.

After class a group had gathered in the hall-way, all talking about Mr. Trout. Sanjita,

Maria, and Janet were among them. I heard Sanji say, "What a spoilsport."

"We did it to him, you know," I blurted out. "If we'd been nice to him, he would have stayed."

"How could we be nice to him?" Maria retorted. "He was so weird."

Janet shook her head. She looked confused. "Why did he do that? He was going to get another bunch of kids in a few days. Besides, you don't just *leave* a job like that, especially without another one lined up."

"Yeah," I said. "Now he's not only humiliated, but poor."

No one knew what to say to that. I just walked away.

When school ended I went straight to Mr. Kingbridge's office. His door was open, and he was busy at his desk. "Mr. Kingbridge?" I said, knocking on the door.

"Come in, Jessi," he replied. "What can I do for you?"

I sat on a chair opposite him. "It's about Mr. Trout. I heard what happened."

He nodded. "Don't you be concerned. He's doing fine and I'll send him your regards if you want. I think you'll like Mr. Bellafatto — "

"Oh, I know I will. It's just that — well . . . oh, it's so terrible, Mr. Kingbridge. He didn't just walk out on you. Us kids drove him out. It's all our fault, most of all *mine!*"

"Why? Because of the Follies skit?"

"That and a million other things." I described all the pranks, including the Balding. I told him what Janet had said about Mr. Trout not having a job now.

Mr. Kingbridge nodded thoughtfully.

Finally I said, "This is so unfair! I mean, I like Mr. Bellafatto and all, but can't we do something to get Mr. Trout back? Can't we give him a second chance? Then, after this week, he may get a nicer class."

With a sigh, Mr. Kingbridge leaned back in his chair. "You know, before I went into education, I was a waiter."

Huh? Had he even *heard* me?

"I thought the restaurant business might be interesting," he went on. "But I kept getting fired. I'd confuse people's food orders. Customers would be mad at me for forgetting to bring ketchup, or extra lemons, whatever — and I would take it all so seriously. Lose sleep over it."

"Well, I guess you weren't meant to do *that* for a living, huh?"

"Nope. Leaving that business was the best thing I ever did." He gave me a warm smile. "Don't worry, Jessica. Someday Mr. Trout will find what he's meant to do. I can guarantee you it won't be teaching sixth grade."

"I . . . I guess," I said.

"Look," he said gently, "your class's behavior was rude and inexcusable. I grant you that. But you didn't cause Mr. Trout to leave. It's not about you, or the other kids. Mostly it's about Mr. Trout himself. Understand?"

I nodded. "Thanks."

I thought about it as I got ready to leave. Mr. Kingbridge had made sense, sort of, but I still wasn't convinced. If Mr. Trout came back, I was sure the class would be nicer to him. Maybe he *was* meant to be a teacher. Maybe he just needed more practice.

I sat down near my locker and drew up a petition that looked like this:

We, the undersigned, request that Mr. Trout be asked back to SMS for a second chance:

_____

_____

_____

_____

_____

_____

Before going home I posted it on the school bulletin board.

That night I composed a letter and typed it out:

Dear SMS students,

One of our teachers, Mr. Trout, has left school. This happened because his students were mean to him. Also because he was insulted by my portrayal in the Follies. Now he has no job. I think he should be invited back to teach. Please sign the petition if you agree.

Thank you.

Sincerely,

Jessica Ramsey

By Friday, seven signatures followed mine on the petition. Six were the other members of the BSC. The seventh looked like this:

TWOUT-MAN
the KLINGON

CHAPTER 14

Saturday

Well, I thought nothing could be funnier than the Sixth-Grade Follies (and I really mean that, Jessi). But I'm telling you, when Charlotte and Becca and Buddy and their friends reach sixth grade, watch out!

Just remember, you saw it all first at my house.

Nyone of us knew what the "BSC Follies" would be like. Most of the "actors" in it — Becca, Charlotte, Buddy Barrett, the Arnold twins, and the rest — had been to the Sixth-Grade Follies the week before.

I was sincerely hoping I wouldn't see any Klingons.

That morning, Mary Anne was getting ready to go to the Barretts' house. She was supposed to sit for Buddy and his two sisters, Suzi and Marnie. (Buddy's eight and mischievous, Suzi's five and cute, and Marnie is an adorable two-year-old.)

Sometimes Mary Anne likes to take her charges back to her house. It's this huge old farmhouse, built in 1795, and it has an enormous barn and an even more enormous yard. It's a great place to sit for kids.

But since Buddy and Suzi were starring in the BSC Follies, Mary Anne was planning to take them all to Charlotte's.

Until the phone rang.

"Mary Anne, it's for you!" her dad called from the kitchen.

Mary Anne, who'd been washing up, went over to the phone.

"Hello," she said.

"Mary Anne, this is an extra-special emergency!" a girl's voice said.

"Charlotte?"

"Yes. Oh, Mary Anne, it's going to rain!"

Mary Anne looked out the kitchen window. It was cloudy and gross-looking. "Uh-oh," she said.

"Can we *please* have the Follies at your house? That way, if it does rain, everybody can go into the barn!"

"Hang on, let me ask."

After some negotiating, Mary Anne got the green light from her dad and stepmom.

And that was how the Official First Annual BSC Follies, produced by Becca Ramsey and Charlotte Johanssen, ended up in the Spier-Schafer yard.

Mary Anne raced over to the Barretts' and brought them to her house. Buddy and Suzi didn't stop giggling the whole way. Marnie looked bewildered.

Next came Charlotte. Then Becca and I arrived.

Before long we had a packed house (packed yard?). All the BSC members were there, plus the Pikes, Mr. and Mrs. Arnold, Daddy and Mama, the Johanssens, and Kristy's family. Even Aunt Cecelia came (although she looked very disapproving of all the noise).

The sky was clearing up, so the kids decided to perform outdoors. Mary Anne's dad and stepmom rushed in and out of the house with kitchen chairs, folding chairs, plastic cartons, anything they could find.

The actors scrambled around, getting ready. Their "set" was a picnic table with a sheet over it, three chairs, and a broken clock on an old card table (borrowed from Mary Anne's barn).

Finally Vanessa Pike shouted out:

"Attention please, attention please!"

Everyone quieted down. The performers (except Vanessa) all disappeared into the barn.

"And now, our intro." Vanessa took a piece of paper from her pocket, unfolded it, and read:

"Welcome to our BSC Follies.

We hope you laugh and have some jollies.

Listen up and follow me,

To a meeting of the BSC."

Then she bowed and said, "Thank you."

Wild applause.

"Boo!" Adam called out.

Mr. Pike leaned over and scolded him. Vanessa stuck her tongue out.

Then, one by one, the kids came out of the barn. First Marilyn Arnold, wearing a visor turned backward and a jogging suit. "Hi, I'm Kristy!" she said.

"Oh, no . . ." Kristy hid her face as everyone burst out laughing.

Vanessa walked out, toting a huge backpack. She had her hair pulled back and fastened by something that looked like a dog bone.

She pulled out a Milky Way bar, stuffed it in her mouth, and said, "Hi, I'm Claudia!"

"Aaaaaugh!" Claudia screamed.

Carolyn followed her, pretending to cry. "I'm — "

Sniff, sniff. "Mary Anne! Boo-hoo-hoo-hoo!"

The *real* Mary Anne turned red as a beet.

Buddy shuffled out of the barn, carrying a football. He walked up behind Carolyn with this embarrassed grin on his face. "Aw, it's all right, Mary Anne," he said in a monotone.

"Hi, Logan," Carolyn said. Then she whispered, *"You're supposed to put your arm around me!"*

Buddy scowled. "This is *dumb!*" he said, stalking away.

Vanessa rushed over to him. It took some convincing, but Buddy walked back onto the "set" to a round of applause.

The show was saved.

Next came Margo, holding a bag of carrots. "I'm Dawn. Yummy, this is my dinner."

Becca came out in a tutu — then promptly ran back into the barn. (She's loud at home, but *very* shy in public!) Finally she came back out as guess who? (I'll give you a hint: she was walking on her toes.)

Squirt broke loose from Mama's arms and

ran toward her, saying, "Baka baka baka!"

When Becca gently handed him back, to a chorus of "Awww's" from the audience, he threw a fit!

Mama finally quieted him down, and the rest of the company emerged from the garage: Suzi with fake glasses (as Mal); Charlotte, in a very fancy outfit, as Stacey; and Haley, bouncing out as Shannon, singing "You-ee you-ee you-ee."

Marilyn/Kristy turned the hands of the rusty old clock to five-thirty and screamed at the top of her lungs, *"ORDER! OR ELSE!"*

We were *convulsing*. Snorting with laughter. Kristy was on the ground.

"NOW FOR OUR OFFICIAL THEME SONG!" Marilyn/Kristy barked. *"NOW! COME ON, SING!"*

Then, together, in teeny little voices, they sang to the tune of the *Sesame Street* song:

"BSC, that is we,

BSC!"

That was as far as they got before dissolving into giggles.

They started again, and finally reached the "won't you smell my Sesame Feet" punchline. Well, that made them crack up completely.

"What does *that* have to do with the Baby-sitters Club?" Jordan Pike complained.

"It was just *funny*, that's all!" Vanessa snapped.

"No, it's not. It's true," Jordan replied. "About your feet."

"*Kids* . . ." Mrs. Pike warned.

The show went on. How was it? Well, *crude*. It didn't have much dialogue, and there weren't any more songs.

But it was one of the funniest plays I have ever seen.

Marilyn/Kristy shouted everything she said. At one point she picked up a stick and wandered off to do some batting practice.

Vanessa/Claudia kept stuffing her face the whole way through, constantly pulling snacks out of her backpack, mumbling all her words. At one point she picked up the clock and said, "This would make a fabulous hat!"

Charlotte/Stacey sniffed disapprovingly. "N.O.M.H. — Not On My Head!"

Margo/Dawn crunched on carrots until she began to look sick.

Suzi/Mal pretended to write in a notebook that had MAL's GRATEST STORY written on the cover. Carolyn/Mary Anne looked over her shoulder and burst into tears every few seconds.

Becca did her imitation of my stretching exercises, breaking into giggles every time she saw me. And Haley/Shannon's singing began to sound like a howling coyote.

Then, after whispering something to Vanessa, Margo yelled, "Brrrring!"

Vanessa picked up the phone and said, "Hello, Baby-sitters Club! Who? The Pike triplets? Sorry, you'll have to call the Monkey-sitters Club."

"Hey!" three voices blurted out.

Oops. I could tell it was going to be Lecture Night at the Pikes.

Well, all the sib squabbling aside, the show was a huge success. We gave them a standing ovation.

Afterward the kids gathered around us, beaming. "Did you like it? Did you like it?"

"GREAT!" Kristy shouted in her best drill sergeant voice. "EXCELLENT!"

"Do you have any more of that candy left over?" Claudia asked with a big grin.

"It was so funny," Mary Anne said, blushing. "I . . . I almost cried."

Logan put his arm around her and said, "Aw, shucks, it's okay."

"Ooooooo!" Haley and Vanessa screamed.

The kids were in hysterics. We were in hysterics.

I only wish I had it on tape.

CHAPTER 15

I learned something from the BSC Follies. It wasn't so horrible to be imitated in a show. It was kind of flattering, in a way. I'd have felt much worse if I had been left out.

Even so, I could not stop thinking about you know who. Mr. Trout.

On Saturday night I had a dream about him. He was standing on stage to receive some kind of award. He was smiling from ear to ear. Everybody was clapping. He had to take four or five bows. Mr. Kingbridge and the two Dollies were behind him, looking on admiringly.

Then, just as he started to give an acceptance speech, the three grown-ups reached over and pulled off his toupee.

The crowd started laughing at him. And his bald head started to grow and grow, swelling like a balloon. He burst into tears and screamed, *"Jessssssiiiiii!"*

I woke up with a start.

The smell of coffee and scrambled eggs wafted up from the kitchen. Mama was humming a song.

I quickly got dressed and went downstairs. Daddy and Mama were both preparing breakfast. I could hear Becca, Squirt, and Aunt Cecelia in the den.

"Hi, baby," Daddy said. "Just in time. Interested in scrambled eggs?"

"Yes, please," I replied.

I sat at the table. Daddy served me my breakfast, then he and Mama sat with me.

"So, what's the word this morning?" Daddy asked.

"Nothing," I said.

Mama started talking about the BSC Follies, but that conversation soon fizzled. Soon the three of us were just munching away silently.

Mama and Daddy exchanged a look.

"A penny for your thoughts," Mama said.

I sighed. I cut my scrambled eggs into tiny pieces.

"A dollar?" Daddy asked. "Inflation, huh?"

I couldn't help laughing. I hadn't planned on dragging my family into the Mr. Trout mess. I'd told them a *little* about him, just that he was strange and wore a toupee, that's all. I guess I'd been too embarrassed to admit what had happened in class.

But right now I needed to talk to someone.

I took a deep breath. "Well, remember that skit about the Klingon?" I began.

I told them everything — the pranks, the Balding, Mr. Trout's reaction. They listened carefully.

"Poor guy," Mama said when I'd finished. "You have some cruel classmates."

Daddy shrugged. "Sounds like he needs to get out of the teaching field."

"That was what Mr. Kingbridge said," I remarked. "But I still feel so guilty about what I did in the show."

Mama and Daddy both looked surprised. "Jessi," Mama said. "He was just an oversensitive man. That's all. You didn't do anything to him that wasn't done to the other teachers."

"I *know*! Everyone always *says* that!" I blurted. "But don't you understand? So what if it's not my fault? *I* still made him feel bad! *My* imitation made him leave town! I just wish I could, like, talk to him."

My eyes were watering again. Mama took my hand. "What would you say if you could talk to him?" she asked.

"Well . . . tell him I'm sorry, and I didn't mean to hurt his feelings. Ask him to come back to the school. Say I was wrong. . . ."

That did it. I buried my head in Mama's shoulder, sniffling away.

Mama rocked me reassuringly. I felt like such a baby — but it was exactly what I needed right then.

"Jessi, honey," Daddy said softly. "Does Mr. Kingbridge know where to reach Mr. Trout?"

"I think so," I replied.

"Then why don't you write to Mr. Trout? Tell him all those things you just told us. That way you'll get it off your chest."

I hadn't thought of that. It wasn't a bad idea. "Okay," I said.

I went up to my room and began.

It was not easy.

How do you write to someone like Mr. Trout — someone who never even said hello to you in the hallway?

I tried, *Please forgive me for being so cruel,* but that sounded too dramatic.

I tried, *I am writing to inform you that I did not intend to hurt your feelings,* but that was too formal.

I threw away at least ten sheets of paper.

Finally I just gave up. But I went back to it Monday night, and every night that week.

By Thursday I had it. I read it aloud seven times, made tons of little corrections, then copied it over.

It went like this:

Dear Mr. Trout,

Hi. I'll bet you didn't expect to hear from me. I hope you read this letter all the way through.

I just want to say I'm sorry. Not that I was involved in the classroom pranks. I wasn't (except for the book dropping), and I thought they were mean. But when I played you in the Follies skit, I thought it was different than that. Just fun. I did not mean to hurt you. I guess I thought it would be all right, because the other teachers did not mind.

But I know everybody is not the same. I understand how it feels to be made fun of.

Please accept my apology. Would you consider returning to SMS? I hope so.

Yours truly
Jessica Ramsey

I showed the letter to my parents. Daddy said he'd *run* back to the school if he got asked as nicely as that.

On Friday morning, I brought it to Mr. Kingbridge. He seemed a little surprised, but he agreed to send it.

A week went by, and I didn't hear a thing.

To be honest, I didn't expect to. But I was happy I had written the letter. And I thought a lot about Mr. Trout — and about what I had done.

Little by little, I began to see that Mr. Kingbridge and Daddy were right. Mr. Trout was too sensitive to be a teacher.

After a couple of weeks with Mr. Bellafatto as a teacher, I understood something else. Mr. Trout had brought a lot of his troubles on himself. He never yelled, never told us we were out of line. He *let* us get out of control. Mr. Bellafatto respected himself, and that made us respect him.

So was I wrong to feel bad? Was it stupid to write Mr. Trout a letter?

I knew that letter by heart. But the more I thought about it, the more I realized part of it was wrong. I *hadn't* thought the skit "would be all right." I had known Mr. Trout wouldn't like it. That bald cap had made me feel creepy the minute I saw it. Why did I go ahead? Because Sanjita and Randy and Mara and all the others wanted me to.

I wanted to fit in. I was worried what they would think of me.

And those were the wrong reasons.

Mr. Trout deserved that apology.

On Friday of that week, I came home to find a letter addressed to me in a tiny, neat handwriting I didn't recognize. I ripped it open, and this is what it said:

Dear Jessica,

Thank you so much for your letter. It meant a lot to me.

I'm sorry you feel so bad. You needn't. I always found you to be a thoughtful, attentive student.

I certainly appreciate your kind invitation to return. But you must understand I simply cannot.

I have applied to a graduate program in advanced computer studies. I'd like to go into research someday. Wish me luck.

My very best to you in the developments of your many talents.

Sincerely,

Michael P. Trout

About the Author

ANN M. MARTIN did *a lot* of baby-sitting when she was growing up in Princeton, New Jersey. She is a former editor of books for children, and was graduated from Smith College.

Ms. Martin lives in New York City with her cats, Mouse and Rosie. She likes ice cream and *I Love Lucy*; and she hates to cook.

Ann Martin's Apple Paperbacks include *Yours Turly, Shirley; Ten Kids, No Pets; With You and Without You; Bummer Summer;* and all the other books in the Baby-sitters Club series.

Look for #76

STACEY'S LIE

When I told Claudia I'd known Robert would be at Davis Park all along, she was pretty ticked off. She went stomping out of the Harbor Store and I had to chase her down the boardwalk. "I can't believe you've been lying to me!" she grumbled when I finally caught up with her.

"I didn't think you'd come if you knew about Robert," I admitted. "I didn't tell you because I really wanted you to come."

The frown stayed on Claudia's face, but her dark eyes softened a bit. "Really?"

"Yes!" I insisted. "Robert will be working all day almost every day."

"Why did you lie?" Claudia asked poutily.

"I just told you!" I cried.

"Aren't we best friends?" said Claudia.

"Of course we are."

"Best friends don't lie and keep secrets. I don't really mind that Robert is here. That's okay. In fact, it's kind of romantic. But it bugs me that you lied."

I put my hand on her arm. "You're right. I'm sorry. Would you have come if I'd told you about Robert?"

A small smile formed on Claudia's lips. "No."

"See?" I cried.

Claudia laughed a little. "You should have told me, anyway."

"Then you wouldn't have come!"

The problem wasn't exactly resolved, but I was glad Claudia wasn't angry anymore. She sighed and shook her head. "I guess it's nice that you wanted me here that badly."

"I did. And I won't lie to you ever again."

"Promise?"

"Promise," I said. "But, listen, Dad doesn't know about Robert, so don't mention him being here. Okay?"

"You shouldn't lie to your father, too," Claudia said.

I raised my eyebrows. "You can't talk! You hid junk food and sneak your Nancy Drew books at night!"

Claudia sighed. "I suppose your right. All right. I won't say anything."

Mysteries:

by Ann M. Martin

More titles... ▶

The Baby-sitters Club titles continued...

Available wherever you buy books...or use this order form.

Scholastic Inc., P.O. Box 7502, 2931 E. McCarty Street, Jefferson City, MO 65102

Please send me the books I have checked above. I am enclosing $_____
(please add $2.00 to cover shipping and handling). Send check or money order - no
cash or C.O.D.s please.

Name _____ Birthdate_____

Address _____

City_____ State/Zip _____

Please allow four to six weeks for delivery. Offer good in the U.S. only. Sorry, mail orders are not
available to residents of Canada. Prices subject to change.

BSC993